THE LOCK

Edward Turbeville

ISBN: 0-9945811-7-3
ISBN-13: 978-0-9945811-7-4

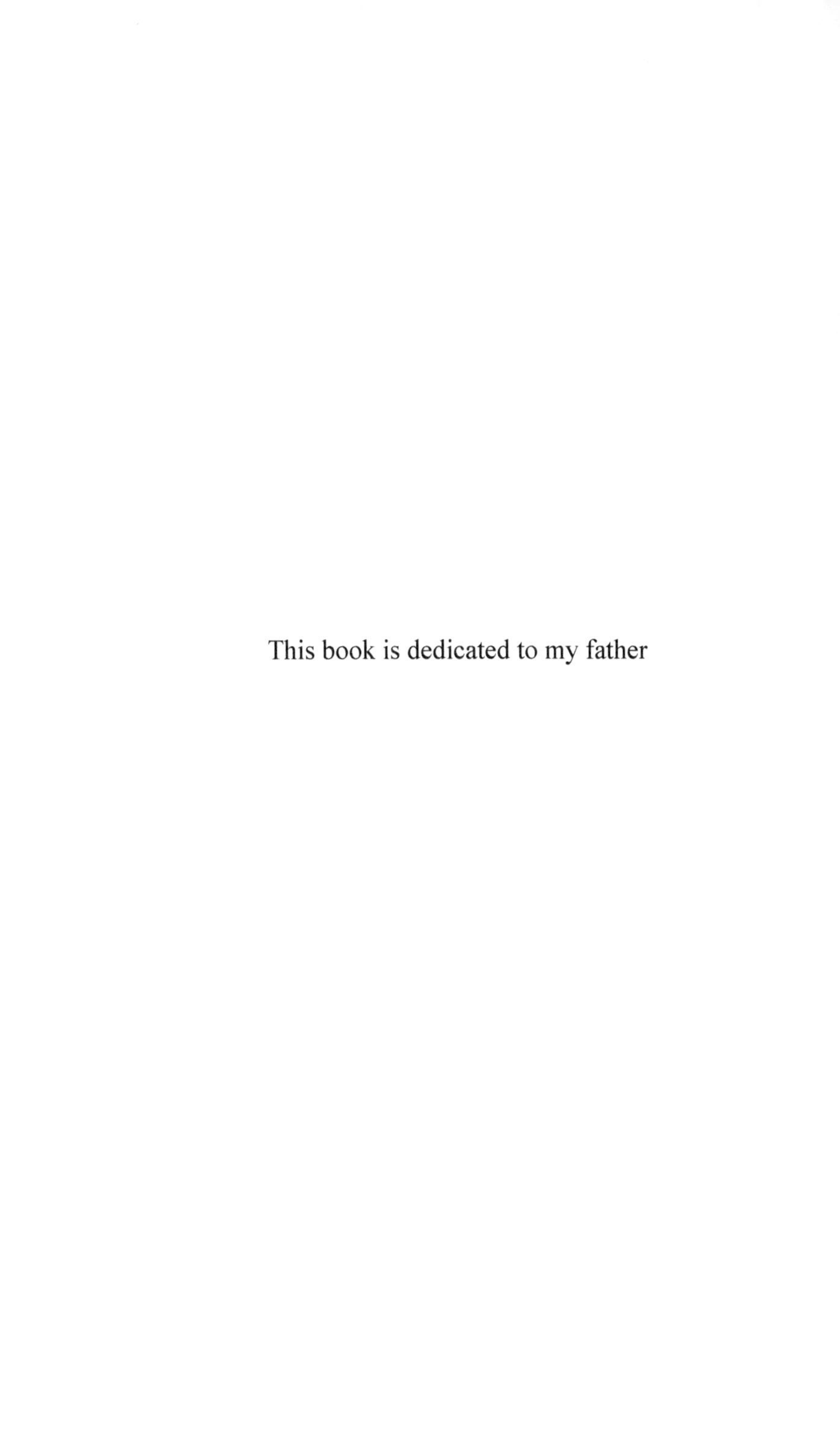

This book is dedicated to my father

Straightest, sublimest of rivers is the long Canal.
I have observed great storms and trembled: I have
wept for fear of the dark.
But nothing makes me so afraid as the clear water
of this idle canal on a summer's noon.

Oxford Canal, by James Elroy Flecker

1

Fine silver wire gleamed in the sunlight as deft fingers wound it around a barbed hook. A twist of feather, coloured thread, a second plume to form a crest. The water was lazy and still around the old narrowboat, the late June afternoon hot and languid, as Perry Beck tied off the fly. He laid it carefully aside, to start on another.

A shadow fell over him. He looked up.

"They say you can open locks."

A girl. Pale, nervous, wearing one of the local school uniforms. She stood on the bank, hesitating to come closer to the young man sitting on the deck.

It was bad enough when word got out, but for a kid to know? Perry said nothing. He reached for another hook and some blue thread. His hands started to wind it around, forming a perfect thin, tiny spool. He needed something to do with his hands. They were restless.

"You have to help me. It's my stepmother. She's going to murder my dad."

There was a sob in the girl's voice and it jarred with the heavy haze of the day. Cow parsley grew thick on the banks, everything was overgrown following the wet of spring and the heat of early summer. Lank, dank, the willows trailing in the water. Perry wanted his peace back. It was the fear in the child's voice that did it. It disturbed him.

"You need the police, then."

He tried to look back down at the fly but his eyes flicked back up and he saw her bite her lip. Saw the desperation there.

"She's got a box. I know she writes stuff in it. A journal, letters. I know it's in there. She wants to kill him, she really does. She only married him for his money. I hate her. I need to get in the box so I've got proof. No one will listen to me otherwise."

It was a child's story, a fantasy. A locked box hiding secrets. A hated stepmother. But the distress was real.

Still Perry said nothing and the girl was silent for a moment, trying to win his trust. "My name's Rose. My dad's Arthur Stanton. He runs the brewery. Please. You're the only one who can help me."

Perry knew of him, of the brewery anyway. He didn't want to feel sorry for the girl but he did.

"I can't help you, Rosie. It's for the police, a matter like that."

She stopped for a moment, looking at him in despair. Not more than twelve, he thought. Too young to have her head filled with fears like this. You run along, he wanted to say.

But then she turned suddenly and left. Rose of the speedwell-blue eyes. Perry wished she had never come, because then he wouldn't have to feel like he had failed her.

"You couldn't do me a favour, could you Perry? I've lost the key to the cashbox and I need to pay wages. Ray's got a spare somewhere but he's not due back for hours."

Perry was sitting at the bar in the Boatswain a couple of days later. It was still early evening and most of the regulars weren't in yet. Late sun streamed in a warm gold beam across the back of the bar, making the bottles and optics shine like a row of potions. The smell of old wood, stale cigarettes and the soft treacly malt of old beer infused the public saloon.

Mary, the publican's wife, pushed a black metal box towards him. She tucked back a strand of fair hair behind her ear. Her cheeks were pink from hauling a crate up from the cellar. Perry would have carried it up for her if she'd asked.

"Drinks on the house if you can get into it, Perry. You'd save me a lot of bother."

Perry regarded the lock, a typical thing of its kind. He delved into his pocket and drew out a short length of wire, about half an unbent paperclip. He reached for the box and quicker than a key could have been turned, clicked it open and pushed it back to Mary.

To the young man sitting at a table a couple of yards away, it appeared that Perry merely brushed the lock and it opened. He was impressed.

"That's quite a party trick you have there."

Perry hadn't realised he had been observed. It was always the way. No wonder word got out. But you had to expect it, at a pub. There was always some drunken fool staggering around losing their keys. Once or twice he'd walked someone home and let them into their own house, if they lived nearby.

The other week he'd opened a bloke's car door for him so he could sit inside and sleep it off for a few hours.

He shouldn't drive in that state of course, so Perry wasn't going to encourage this by hot wiring the vehicle as well, something else he could have done.

Anyway, what could you do when someone asked? When it was no real skin off Perry's nose, and twenty quid and hours of waiting if they had to call up a locksmith.

Perry looked at the dark-haired man at the nearby table. He was young, about his own age. Early twenties maybe. Any similarity ended there though, because the other man was gown. A student, from one of the university colleges, as opposed to someone from the town. Gown and town rarely mixed. Funny place for him to be drinking, given all the colleges had their own bars with cheap beer for students.

"Join me for a beer?"

It would be churlish to refuse yet the only other polite option would be to make his excuses and leave. But Perry didn't want to go just yet. He was waiting for Priscilla, one of the barmaids, to start her shift.

"May as well."

The other man introduced himself. "Martin Harcourt."

"Perry Beck. Student, are you?"

Martin raised his eyebrows at the inquiry, more of an accusation than a question, and then laughed. "When I feel like opening my books. I'm local too though. I grew up here, or near here. My family live in Tackley." It was a village a few miles to the north of town.

"Nice place." Perry took another gulp of his ale.

Martin found himself intrigued by the local man. Perry Beck was weirdly colourless and nondescript, yet there was that almost preternatural ability with a lock.

Martin had heard the term "rubbing a lock" before but had never really understood what it meant.

Until he saw Perry's display of the dark arts.

His eyes were unusual too. Martin didn't spend much time analysing other blokes' physical features, he wasn't interested that way. But where you'd expect a muddy colour to match everything else, they were a distinct grey-green. A brighter colour than they should have been, Martin thought.

"So where did you learn the lock thing?" Martin asked.

"It's just a knack."

It was a deliberately evasive answer. "You're not a locksmith, then?"

Perry shook his head.

"Never considered it?"

There was a flicker of something in the greenish eyes. "You need certificates and stuff. A licence."

Martin had spent enough vacations doing work experience in his uncle's law practice to recognise that guarded look. He'd seen it any amount of times among a particular fraternity.

"Form?" Martin asked, referring to a criminal record.

"Just a stupid kid." Perry didn't want to think about it, it had blighted his life long enough.

Martin drained his pint and signalled to Mary for two more. "If you were a kid it's probably long expired by now. I could check it out for you. My uncle's a solicitor."

Perry said nothing. He saw that Priscilla had arrived behind the bar. He wanted to ask her out one of these days but it was too early yet. For now he liked it enough when she spoke to him, and she was something to look at. Irish looking, he thought, with black hair and dark eyes, though her accent was English.

She was talking to Damon, Mary's brother, who had recently come to stay at the pub. He'd been living overseas. Damon's hair was too long, he wore faded velvet jackets and his pupils were like pinpricks. Perry had his number and he could tell Priscilla did too. So he wasn't unduly worried by her conversation with him.

Martin observed Perry observing Damon and Priscilla, and guessed where the land lay. She came over to them, bringing them two fresh pints. "Awful, isn't it?" she said. "I was just talking about it with Damon. You wouldn't think such a thing would happen in a quiet little place like this, would you?"

Neither Martin nor Perry had any idea what the barmaid was talking about. Martin made this known. "So what's up?"

Priscilla frowned, her pert and pointy little face showing surprise.

"The brewery bloke, of course. Arthur Stanton. Shot dead last night. Murder, not suicide. Just outside his home. Point blank range, they said."

You have to help me...

Perry stood up. He felt sick and wanted to be back on his boat.

"I've got to get going."

He left, not saying goodbye to either of them, and oblivious to the greetings of some regulars who passed him on the way out.

No one will listen to me...

He wasn't going to think about the kid. She wasn't any of his concern. She was someone else's problem. What could he have done anyway? Like as not there was nothing incriminating in the box anyway. What sort of an idiot would write down those sorts of plans in black and white?

You're the only one who can help me...

The houseboat creaked and gently rocked as he stepped onto it. It was a cocoon. Inside it was Perry's world. He owned it. It was all his. He'd named it Emerald, after his mother.

He'd never had a father. No one ever spoke of him and so he'd never asked. Perry had only guessed that he might have been a dub - a lock picker - because they gave him locks to play with as early as he could remember.

A couple of them spoke of his mother but he was never quite sure how she was related to them. Everyone was "uncle" and "aunt" and even "grandpa", though they weren't anything of the kind.

His earliest memory wasn't of his mother. How could it be? She'd died before he was a year old. A great loss, Old Owen had said once or twice. They said she was beautiful, with emerald eyes.

Perry thought that she might have loved him. For the rest of them, life was more about survival than love.

The lock and the picks put into his hands were his first memories. Learning to play them, much like a violin. Learning by trial and error and perhaps also instinct the perfect pressure, speed and rhythm.

Someone, it might have been Jake the Flick, had tossed him currants each time he picked it. Or so he thought, because even as his hands itched these days to hear that click, that solution, he sometimes felt a craving for currants.

It was so easy. Too easy, even when they gave him other locks. A kid spends its whole life at that age learning to interact with its physical environment. No wonder he picked it up like he had, genes or no genes.

What if they'd given him a piano, a paintbrush? Bribed him to master those? Would he feel the same urge in his fingers to play a pleasing sequence of notes or paint a beautiful scene to find release?

But they'd put different instruments in his hands. And so the rub was his stroke, the click was his music, the lock's release his release.

2

Hauling sacks of compost was hot work and Perry was glad the day was cooler than the previous one. It got harder as the stacks got higher: they'd had a bulk delivery the previous day and it all needed to be moved.

Barnaby Goodlock, co-owner of the nursery, stood up and wiped his brow, wide and sun-bronzed. Both men were muscled from all the manual labour involved, but Barnaby had a broader build than Perry's wiry strength.

"What's all this, then?" Perry asked. The sacks had Spanish or some other foreign words on them.

Barney rolled his eyes. "Special soil, for Frankie's exotics. Cost an arm and a leg."

The couple had met in South America somewhere, backpacking. When they'd started Goodlock Nursery Frankie had wanted to run a sideline in rainforest exotics. Collectors would pay a premium for them, she argued, and she'd largely been right. The problem was that there wasn't a huge amount of collectors. It also meant one of the greenhouses was given over as a hothouse but plant-for-plant they made tenfold what petunias and pumpkin seedlings did.

They also cost tenfold to import, but Frankie insisted the margins would improve as they grew the market for them.

Flamingo flowers, Chameleon vine, Peacock Poinciana. The names were far more colourful, in Perry's view, than the struggling specimens under glass. He didn't see how there could ever be much of a demand. Most of the orders seemed to be from Cornwall, for where else could you hope to keep such a thing alive? Perry had never been to Cornwall but he'd been told it was warm enough there to grow palm trees. Not like Oxfordshire, where the first frost would have done for the lot of them.

It wasn't for him to say anything though. Albeit he suspected that Barney felt much the same way.

Perry had been late arriving to work that morning because the police had stopped by the canal. He should have guessed they'd come. After all they were asking questions of everyone in the area, and Perry had form. Paint a man, as they said.

Perry didn't want them on his boat, polluting it with their heavy tread, so he had stepped off it onto the bank. He had his own reasons enough to be wary of coppers. "Just a few questions." "Routine inquiries." Little notebooks and pencils, times and dates. Then they stitched you up.

They didn't know about the kid visiting him of course, and he wasn't going to tell them. That was her business, not his.

He could tell from their tone and the questions that they had few leads. They weren't targeting the wife yet anyway, as they didn't even ask if he knew her. Perry had never met the brewery owner either - now "the deceased" in police talk.

Perry had nothing to tell them and they didn't seem to know what to ask, so they soon moved on and he made his own way to the nursery.

It was good land they had, Barney and Frankie. Good soil. Affordable too because it was no good for building, edging onto floodplains. You could run a small market garden on the side if you didn't mind being flooded out every few years. The flood risk kept the land value down. Otherwise in this part of the country, so close to the city, you'd have needed to be a millionaire to put up a shack there.

Frankie appeared with cheese rolls and cans of beer. "Got to feed my workers," she said. She had long hair, all plaited into tiny braids, from a recent plant-buying trip to Costa Rica or somewhere. Perry supposed she was attractive enough but she wasn't his type. Like Barney she was tanned from working outside, her lean shoulders exposed to the sun under her dungarees.

"Ta." Barney took a roll and handed another to Perry, cracking open the beer.

"Thirsty work?" Frankie asked Perry.

"Somewhat."

They were nearly done, and then there was a load of statuary to move onto a display. It wasn't in either Barney's or Frankie's taste, but customers kept asking for it. Fake marble planters with cherubs, ornamental bird baths, stone animals to dot around a suburban garden. So far they'd drawn the line at gnomes.

"Perry had the police round earlier," Barney told Frankie. "Asking about that Stanton man's shooting."

"I should say it was suicide," Frankie said. She was dismissive of it. "Probably had business problems."

"They never found a gun, so it was said."

Frankie looked scornful. "Who said?"

"Dilys," Barney told her.

"I might have guessed."

Dilys Jones cleaned at the pub in the mornings, bringing gossip along with her mops.

"Nasty business though," Barney said, biting into his cheese roll. "Not what you'd expect in this neck of the woods. Guns."

Frankie shrugged. "There's always guns. Loads of farmers have them. You of all people ought to know that, Barney." This was a reference to Barney having been to agricultural college.

"Not that type though. It was a pistol, so Dilys said."

"As if she would know."

"She works at the Stantons'. The wife - the widow - probably told her," Barney pointed out.

The widow. It gave Perry an uneasy feeling. He wondered how the girl was. He reminded himself that it wasn't his problem and tried not to think about it.

Back on his boat, a surprise even less welcome than the police. He should have guessed they'd track him down. They were like fleas, you could never shake them for long.

"Beck my lad. It's a fine set up you've got yourself here. Quiet and cosy, like."

King John Lochinvar, as he styled himself. Hale, hearty and black-bearded, though with more of a grizzle in it now than Perry remembered. It had been a few years but it might well have been yesterday.

Behind King John loped Old Owen, his shadow and henchman. Old Owen looked unchanged, but he'd been pale and elderly looking for as long as Perry had known him.

"You can't stop here," Perry said. He knew why they had come. He had always known they'd come back and start pestering him again.

"A fine way to greet family! For we're all family from long back, aren't we, uncle?" This was addressed to Old Owen, though he wasn't King John's uncle or even a relation.

"Speak your piece," Perry said. He just wanted them gone. They were part of his past and they were nothing but trouble.

"Now, now, my lad, we'd hoped for a warmer welcome than that. Particularly with what we've got to offer you." King John beamed but there was a wily glint in his eye.

A job. Perry had guessed the minute he saw them that King John had come to claim the hands he'd trained.

It was indeed a job, an "easy little number with good pickings in it for you, Beck my lad."

"It's not what I do anymore," Perry told them bluntly. It wasn't what he had ever willingly done.

"See, we tried to train up the boy Joe to help out, but he's not got the knack has he, uncle? None of your charm, Beck."

Perry had no idea who the boy Joe was and didn't ask.

"It's not a good time," he said. "There's been cops round here. Cove done in with a dag." Despite himself he slipped back into their familiar cant.

King John drew his breath between his teeth in a whistle. "And what be they sniffing round here for? You in the suds, Beck lad?"

"All clean. Just routine, so far as I know."

"That's good then. That's all good." King John looked around himself, eyeing the direction of the cabin. "Been waiting here a while for you, haven't we?"

He was angling for a drink. Old Owen hovered behind him. "That we have," he said.

Perry hadn't got any beer on the boat and he didn't want them accompanying him to the Boatswain. It was his patch and he didn't want to be explaining these two.

The White Stag would be more in their line anyway. It was half a mile walk the other way, next to the canal. It attracted more day trippers and more transients, and with that more shady kinds of trade ferried up and down the canal.

"There's nothing here, but we'll go for a drop nearby," Perry said. He'd buy them a round then shake them off.

"Quiet sort of place, I trust?" King John asked. He meant were there police sniffing around.

"Quiet enough."

King John suddenly slapped Perry on the back. "You're a good lad, Beck. Wouldn't turn your back on the Company, would you? Just as I was saying to uncle here earlier. He doesn't forget who his friends are, does he?"

"Ah," Old Owen said.

Perry had flashes of those earliest years. He wasn't sure exactly who had raised him after his mother died, but the main female figure had been Black Bessie. Bessie wasn't black, she was large, fat and white. Her daughter Tina was mixed race as her dad, one of Bessie's many gentlemen friends, was West Indian. Tina wasn't around much, living mainly with her father.

The rest of the Company stayed in various houses, often on the move. A couple of them had vans but they weren't much of a travelling community in terms of living on the road. Moving was often sudden, swift, in the night.

But again, Perry was remembering that from later. As a small child he really didn't recall much at all. Just the locks and the picks, and a scratchy brown carpet that he seemed to be sitting on for hours.

Then everything had changed when Bessie got into trouble for something and the Social stepped in. Five-year-old Perry was taken away from everyone he knew and put with a foster family. He didn't remember minding much about it at first. There were too many new things to take his attention, including a very nice, hairy dog.

That house wasn't for long though, because then he went somewhere else, and passed through several more places. Sometimes there were other kids his own age he could play with. Sometimes there were older ones who were mean to him.

There was a spell in a children's home when one foster mother had to go into hospital. No one had ever told Perry what happened to her but he had long forgotten her name. He got used to packing his little case with his few possessions and hand-me-down clothes and moving on.

There was school too, and that was an ordeal. The foster kids usually stuck together; they were always picked on by the others. You grew a pair of fists or you hid away at break time. Somehow through all this Perry managed to learn to read and write. He liked books but he was never given access to very many. "They always rip them to pieces," he'd heard someone saying of foster kids. It was true, some of the other kids did rip books up. They were useful for paper planes and other purposes. And if you couldn't read them, and many of the kids couldn't, why not rip them up?

3

Perry took a collection of silk flies round to Mary who sold them for him at the bar. It wasn't a roaring trade but a few quid was better than nothing.

"They're so pretty," Priscilla said, admiring one with iridescent blue-green feather wings. "You should make necklaces from them, Perry. They'd sell like hotcakes down the market. You'd have to take the hooks out though."

They wouldn't be flies then, Perry thought. They'd just be ornamental bits of feather and thread. As fishing flies, they had a purpose.

"At least you should sell them as lucky fishing flies," Priscilla continued. "Anglers are superstitious, aren't they? I bet they'd pay more if they thought there was a gypsy's charm on them."

Perry forbore to point out that he wasn't a gypsy. People got the idea that since he lived on a boat, he must have Romany blood. He didn't really know what his blood was, but he doubted it was anything like that. Not if King John, Bessie and the rest of the crew were anything to go by.

It had taken him three rounds to finally shake the two of them off last night, though he wasn't convinced that King John had taken no for an answer. The White Stag had been full of the usual crowd, and they'd been huddled around a little table in a quiet nook, with King John explaining the plans. It was almost like the good old days, except they'd never been good.

Perry had also felt uneasy when he spotted Damon across the room, though Damon didn't see him. There was only one reason someone like Damon would bother going drinking in a dive like the Stag, when he had free beer on tap in his sister's pub. Perry watched Damon meeting up with a tattooed bloke with dreadlocks and talking with him briefly. There was an exchange, and then they both left. It was crudely done, Perry had considered.

He tuned back into King John, still rattling on about his grand scheme. They'd been casing a jeweller of all things, in Witney. Old Owen could break the safe but they needed to get into the place.

There'd be all sorts of alarms, Perry had pointed out. It wasn't like the old days, everything was wired up now. Especially a jeweller's.

King John had dismissed these concerns. They had a new fellow called Colin who managed all that. An electronics whizz-kid, King John described him as. Colin had said the type of alarm was child's play to disconnect, and that had been enough to convince the others. Baubles were much easier to fence. The electronics trade, the Company's speciality, was declining. Cars all came with CD players these days and everyone wanted a brand new TV. Only a junkie would filch that gear now, the returns just weren't worth it unless you were desperate.

"There's no respect for anything older," King John had said, shaking his head sadly.

"No respect," Old Owen had echoed.

Either way, Perry wasn't interested in helping out. He was content with his situation. He could always do with more money - the boat was going to need a new engine come winter - but he wasn't desperate enough to get embroiled in one of King John's schemes.

"You'll have to find someone else." Perry refused to help. They must have been using someone else all these years.

"Like I said, we tried training up the boy. But he's not got your touch, Beck." The jeweller would be a major job for them and they didn't want to take any risks.

But Perry was resolute. "It's not for me."

Now he was rid of them, sitting peacefully by himself in the Boatswain, he found himself idly wondering how Priscilla might react if he gave her a diamond necklace. Likely she'd guess it was stolen.

Mary joined Priscilla behind the bar. It was quiet that evening so they hardly needed two people serving. Ray had taken the night off and had gone to the greyhounds with a friend. "I was just telling Perry that he ought to sell his fishing flies down at the market. Don't you think so? You know what, Frankie Goodlock's got a stall at the Midsummer Festival. I bet she'd put some out for you if you asked, Perry."

"It's a good idea," Mary agreed. "That crowd would pay more than anglers."

The Midsummer Festival was a hippy, eco event with folk bands and people selling joss sticks, tie-dye t-shirts and purported organic goods. Frankie had hopes of drumming up business for her exotic plants under the guise of "mystic flora". Perry, like Barney, had been planning to give the whole affair a wide berth.

"So are you going this year then, Perry?" Priscilla asked him.

"I suppose I might be."

Just as he was working out how he might turn this into some kind of date, he saw Priscilla perk up at the entrance of another customer, her attention immediately deserting Perry.

Perry glanced behind him. It was the university student from the other night, Martin. He felt no rancour at the other man so easily attracting Priscilla's interest. Perry could bide his time. If and when Martin showed no interest, Priscilla would give up and then Perry could make his own attempt. It was just a question of being patient. So he figured, anyway.

Martin greeted him and pulled up the stool next to him. "What are you having?"

"I'm alright with this one," Perry said, indicating his half full pint.

He meant that he didn't need another drink, not yet anyway, but Martin chose to interpret it to mean more of the same. "Get him another one of those, and I'll have a lager," he said to Priscilla who flashed him a smile and went to pull the pints.

"Not gone down for the holidays, then?" she asked Martin as she put the drinks down in front of the two men. The university had just broken up for the year and the town was emptied of students. They'd be replaced by tourists, most of them day trippers coming up in coaches from London.

"No. I'm more or less local, and my uncle's given me some vacation work in his legal practice." Martin took a draught of the lager.

Priscilla was turning on the flirtation. "That must be interesting. Any exciting cases?"

"We're representing the widow of the bloke that got shot," Martin told her. "Just probate, for now anyway."

"For now?" Priscilla had sharp ears. "Are they going to charge her? Did she do it?"

Perry shifted uncomfortably on his stool. He was uneasy with the subject. It was all anyone seemed to talk about: who shot Arthur Stanton?

Martin grinned. "I couldn't say even if I knew. Client confidentiality and all that. But truthfully, your guess is as good as mine."

Priscilla gave a shiver and Perry noted that she wasn't a very good actress. "Horrible to think of," she said. "Makes you feel unsafe in your bed, thinking a murderer is still at large."

"I shouldn't think they'd come after you," Martin said.

It wasn't quite what Priscilla wanted to hear, neither his words nor his tone. She tossed her head, turned and left them to serve another customer.

"Had a kid, didn't he?" Perry asked, then immediately regretted doing so. He didn't want to know and he didn't want become involved.

"A girl, yes. Poor kid. I can't imagine her and the stepmother get on like much of a house on fire," Martin said. "Nasty business all round."

Nasty indeed. If the stepmother ditched her, and well she might, the kid might end up like Perry had. In the system. It was even worse for a girl.

Another fellow strode into the bar. Barney. He greeted Perry and offered him a drink. Perry declined, but introduced him to Martin.

"Barnaby Goodlock." They shook hands, which all seemed a bit formal to Perry. But the two others were cut from the same cloth. Private schools, university education. It was a club that Perry would never belong to.

"Not Goodlock Nursery, are you?" Martin asked, taking a lucky guess. "I pass that on the way to work."

"That's me. Or us. My wife Frankie and I own the place."

The conversation turned to Martin's mother, who was apparently a keen amateur horticulturalist, and her garden. Martin had absorbed some of this lore. Perry tuned out at the words "herbaceous border". His mind drifted.

It was doubtful that Martin could have related much more about the murder investigation because the police seemed to have few leads. The wife was typically the primary suspect, but Arthur Stanton had been known for being a hard businessman so the Brewery was an angle they couldn't rule out.

Arthur Stanton wasn't from Oxfordshire originally. He had been born in the Midlands where his family had hailed from for generations. His father and grandfather had owned a small industrial works but times were getting tough. Arthur inherited it at a reasonably young age, since heart disease ran in the Stanton line and its menfolk rarely made old bones.

He sold it, moved south, and bought a small, struggling brewery. He changed the name to Stantons and started building it up. Among other things his previous factory had made beer dispensing equipment, which gave Arthur a foot in the door with a couple of pub chains around Birmingham and Wolverhampton. Thanks to this and a certain ruthless streak, Stantons prospered.

He married a local girl who bore him a daughter. He wanted a son to continue the Stanton line, and pass the business down as his own father and grandfather had done. He could be patient. After all, kids didn't come to order. But no son came, and just before the first Mrs Stanton, Rose's mother, was due to go in for some medical tests, she fell sick.

Six months later Arthur was a widower with a small daughter. He eventually married again, to a woman still young enough to beget the Stanton heir. The years went by and business became more demanding and more complicated as Stantons expanded. No heir came, and a certain sense of bitterness had befallen Arthur Stanton.

The newspapers reported some of this, other parts were local knowledge gleaned from people like Dilys Jones.

It may have been at the back of Arthur's mind to divorce Sybil, go back north and find himself a heartier wench from his hometown to fulfil his aim. Third time lucky and so on. He may even have been starting to look up divorce lawyers in the phone directory. But if this was the case no one could know, because late one night someone shot him, and his secrets died with him.

Everyone had their secrets. Backgrounds they kept hidden. Despite all the years he spent with the Company, Perry didn't even know all the other members' real names or where they were from.

He was nine years old, and he'd been in the system for four years, when the Company came to retrieve him. Black Bessie was back on the scene along with all the usual suspects.

Literal suspects, for most of the robberies in the area.

Bessie had managed to get custody of Perry. She'd conned a well-meaning but naive social worker that she was Perry's aunt, and that she was sufficiently reformed following a spell in Holloway to care for him once again. The social workers had too many higher risk kids on their hands as it was, so they were glad to offload any cases they could.

Perry was older now, there wasn't any abuse or violence recorded in his file, so back into the care of the Company he went. He only had the vaguest memories of most of them, though he faked affection for "Aunty Bessie" in front of the social workers because anything was better than the current home he was in.

It was great being in his own place, not a guest anymore. Not having to worry that someone else would nick or trash his stuff. What there was of it, anyway. He could eat what he liked and when he liked, with no one threatening him with a belt for taking too much jam, or forcing him to eat cold baked beans three days in a row.

For a little while, Perry was in Paradise.

4

Now it was Martin who showed up at Perry's boat. Everyone was turning up there these days. He'd have to find new moorings if he wanted any peace. It was grey that day with a cold wind and Perry was feeling a restlessness that tying flies couldn't assuage.

"I've got a proposition for you," Martin said. "A job, well more of a favour really. There's two hundred quid in it though. Cash."

It would go a good way towards the new engine, so Perry was prepared to listen.

It turned out to be a divorce. A pretty vicious one. The man had beaten her up, kicked her out and changed the locks. The lawyers and courts were supposed to be sorting out all the financial settlement, but the problem was he'd kept some photos.

"He's a nasty piece of work. He took them of her a few years ago, you can imagine the sort of thing. Bedroom stuff. Now he won't give them to her. Leverage. He wants her to accept less than she's owed."

Don't get involved, was Perry's first instinct. But after turning down King John and the jewellery job, he'd been giving more of a mind to money. Two hundred quid. It was tempting.

"You can't get them back in the regular way?"

"It's the exposure. She's a teacher, respected in the community, does the church flowers, that sort of thing. This will ruin her career. It shouldn't of course, there's nothing illegal about adult photos, but you know how it is."

Perry didn't really know how it was. He'd never even owned a camera. He took Martin's word for it.

"What happens when he discovers they're gone?" Perry asked.

"There's not a lot he can do. He can hardly make a big song and dance about it with the police, given he was using them for blackmail."

Blackmail. It was an ugly word for an uglier crime. One which even the Company would shrink from stooping to.

"It's totally fine if it's not for you. I just thought I'd ask. She's a nice woman, she doesn't deserve this," Martin said.

It was the cry for help more than the money that tipped Perry over the edge. "I'll see what I can do," he said.

Martin gave him all the details. To Perry it seemed absurdly easy. The bloke went to Rotary on a Wednesday night. No alarms. No dogs. A couple of Yale locks. A locked drawer. "She didn't know what kind that one was, she said sort of an 'old fashioned key'. We're both novices in this area, I'm afraid."

It felt like taking candy from a kid.

Wednesday came and Perry made his way there. It was close to the solstice so he'd had to wait until past ten o'clock for a proper cover of darkness. Adrenalin sharpened his reflexes and he made his way up the driveway, melting against the shadows of bushes lest any neighbours were twitching at their curtains.

Stealth and soft soles were second nature to him from his days with the Company. But he could have done this one with a flashing light and tap shoes for all there was any danger.

Perry slipped inside like a shadow. The floor was parquet and the house smelt of stale cigars. He found the bureau easily, exactly as described. The drawer lock was nothing to him, he had tools but he could have done it just as quickly with a hair grip. He really didn't know why people bothered with these old locks in antique desks, they served no practical purpose. Maybe to keep a small child out, assuming that small child wasn't a five-year-old Perry Beck.

The envelope was there as they had said it would be. Opening it, he found both photos and negatives - a cursory glance at the images showed him that it was the correct material. He wasn't interested in going through them.

He rifled through the other drawers in case there was anything else but couldn't find anything of note.

Replacing everything exactly as it had been, save for the envelope, he slipped back outside again to make his way home.

It was all so easy. So easy that he felt paranoid that it must be all some kind of set up. But no one followed him: there were no flashing lights, no knocks on his door, nothing.

The next day he took the envelope, as instructed, to Martin's uncle's office. It was near the centre of town and he had no problem finding it.

Martin met him in reception. "Come through." Perry was led into an inner room, still nervous that it was all a trick. An older man sat behind the desk. It was a typical solicitor's office. Perry had been in a couple in his time.

"My uncle Jeff," Martin said. "This is Perry Beck, the guy I told you about."

Jeff Harcourt extended a hand, intending to shake Perry's hand, but Perry, thinking he wanted the envelope, handed it straight to him. There was a momentary awkwardness. The solicitor checked the contents briefly and raised his eyebrows.

"I can't officially condone the method, Martin, but there's no doubt we've got the result we wanted."

Martin was elated. "She's going to be over the moon. I can't thank you enough, Perry."

Perry was feeling a bit like Robin Hood. He mumbled something non-committal. Martin gave him a wad of notes that Perry didn't even dare count. He felt like he would jinx it.

As he was leaving, he passed a woman entering the reception. She was dressed head to toe in a brownish-pink shade, with lots of frills around the edging. A matching hat with a small net veil half covered one eye. She tottered past Perry on high heels, and dropped some papers as she did so. He picked them up for her and she twittered her thanks.

"No trouble," Perry said, and the woman gave him an oddly simpering smirk.

Her face was silly looking all over: false eyelashes, rouged cheeks, too much lipstick in a peach shade that clashed with her dress. Skinny bit of mutton, Perry thought.

As he left he heard the receptionist greet her. "Mrs Stanton, welcome. Mr Harcourt will be with you in just a moment."

So this was the stepmother. No wonder the kid couldn't stand her.

Nonetheless, Perry didn't think she looked capable of holding a gun and shooting someone.

Hiring someone else to do it? Maybe.

Flush with cash and feeling like a small celebration was due, Perry made his way back towards the canal. He remembered he'd promised to help Ray and Mary with some crates. Ray had done his back in the previous week and couldn't lift.

Ray greeted Perry by the cellar door. "Don't know what we'd do without you. My back's shot and I can't have Mary trying to do it all."

He was about ten years older than Mary, a jovial bloke in his mid-forties and every inch the publican.

"You win anything the other day, at the track?" Perry asked. He had half a mind to put a bet on himself. A tenner ought to do it.

"Not a ha'penny. It's all rigged, all nobbled. It's not what it used to be. They've all got bent vets and drugs these days. It's a mug's game."

Perry wondered how much Ray had lost. More than he'd ever admit to Mary, that was certain.

Dilys Jones came past, carrying her cleaning equipment, wearing overalls with her hair tied up in its usual scarf. She was only Mary's age but she dressed like an old woman when she worked. He liked her though, she had a good heart.

"Keeping well, Perry?" she greeted him. She was from Wales originally and still had the accent.

"Not so bad. You?" he asked her, dragging another crate behind the bar so Ray could start refilling the fridge with bottles.

"Same. Least when my customers aren't dropping dead on me."

Ray overheard. "You mean the Stanton fellow? You not still working for his missus then."

"Madam has dispensed with my services." Dilys gave an imitation of a prissy English voice as she said this.

"I'm sorry to hear that, Dilys," Ray said.

"Don't you worry about me. It was one morning a week, I've got others lined up to take the hours. It's little Rose I feel sorry for. Stanton's kid. Got no one now, has she? It's not like Madam Sybil's going to want anything to do with her. Once the solicitors have sorted the will she'll be out of there."

"D'you reckon she did it then?" Ray asked.

"No, and more's the pity. I'd like to see her banged up with Big Lil and the girls." Dilys gave a cackle of laughter as she rinsed and dried a stack of ashtrays. "Be a sight, that would. Stuck up cow. No, it will be someone to do with the business. Likely a customer he screwed over. He wasn't exactly popular, was he?"

Ray, who was one of the brewery's customers, agreed. "Always putting the squeeze on. I'm surprised someone hadn't done him in before now."

Later, when Dilys had finished her shift and sat down to her half of cider, Perry was still hanging around. He had the idea that if he mentioned Rose's visit to her, he'd have done right by the kid and it would be off his conscience.

"Out with it then, Perry," Dilys said. She cut into his thoughts while he was still forming them. She often second guessed people. Far too astute to do what she did, really. She overheard way too much and was eerily adept at filling in any blanks.

Perry sat down at the table by the Welsh woman. Ray had gone out the back to do something and would be away for a while. "The Stanton kid," Perry began. "She dropped by the canal the other week. Had a story about her stepmother doing her dad in. Before it happened, I mean."

Dilys raised her eyebrows and tapped her cigarette into the newly-cleaned ashtray. She brought it to her lips again before replying. "You been to the cops about this?" She looked at him, thinking. "Of course you haven't, you're the last one who'd do that, aren't you? So what did she want from you. Something opened?"

She was making this easy for Perry. "A box, she said. Claimed it had proof in it. I took it for a kid's story." He regretted this now, he could admit that to himself. "I should have opened it, maybe. He might be here now, if..."

Dilys cut into him. "Don't you think like that. This isn't on your head, Perry. Like I said, it wasn't Sybil Stanton that did it, for all the fuzz have been sniffing around her. I know that box too. Got a funny looking lock, it has. She keeps it under her dressing table."

"You think I'm alright then, not saying anything?" Going to the cops with information was such anathema to Perry that as law-abiding as he was these days, every cell in his body revolted against it.

"The man's dead, it's not going to make any difference to anyone now, is it? You leave be. Someone's got a gun after all. Let the coppers handle it their own way. They can always jemmy it open, if they want to."

Jemmying the box. It got him remembering the old times again, and all the skills he had been taught.

It was Jake the Flick rather than Black Bessie who took over most of Perry's raising. Perry was supposed to go to school, but after another term or so the Company moved again and didn't bother to re-enrol him anywhere else.

He didn't miss it. Irregular schooling left him at the bottom of the class, and though he'd learned to use his fists, the playground had remained an ordeal. Instead there was Jake to look out for him and teach him everything. He showed him all kinds of different things, how to get about unseen, how to open doors, windows, hatches, how to always find a way in and a way out. He was about ten years older than Perry and became like a big brother.

Jake wasn't much of a dub himself, but he helped Perry hone his skills until locks sang and slipped under his lightest touch.

Sometimes Perry was even quicker with a wire than a key. Once you knew what you were feeling for, the barrels dissolved to liquid.

"He's pure gilt, this one," Jake had told the others, and Perry felt proud for the first time ever. No one had ever praised him for anything. He'd never been good at anything before nor known that he could be.

5

There was a shifty looking fellow hanging around Goodlock Nursery when Perry arrived for work that afternoon. He had greying hair that needed a cut and a shabby tweed hat. If Perry hadn't known better he might have thought he was one of King John's lot.

Barney was out making deliveries so it was just Frankie there. She saw Perry looking at the visitor.

"That's Grover. He wanted some work but I've said I've got nothing for him. Says he was laid off from the brewery not long ago."

Why was he hanging around then? She was too much of a soft touch, Frankie. Perry could tell without even speaking to the man that he was as crooked as they came. She should have sent him packing the minute he showed up.

As if reading Perry's mind, Frankie spoke to the man. "You'd best be off, Grover. We've got nothing for you, but if we need any extra hands, I'll give you a bell."

Grover turned to go but then she stopped him. "You'd better leave me your number then, hadn't you?"

Grover looked confused for a moment, then took the pencil Frankie held out and wrote down a number. If Frankie had any sense she'd crumple it up and toss it,

Perry thought. Anyway it was none of his concern. His nerves were still on edge, he thought, from King John Lochinvar's arrival.

When the man had finally gone, Perry took out the box of silk flies he had brought with him. "Priscilla thought I might show you these. Said you might be able to sell some down at the Festival."

Frankie took one out, taking care not to prick herself on it. "They're beautiful, Perry. So delicate. Do you just make them by hand?"

He nodded. "They're not so hard, once you've made a few."

A couple of them he'd crafted to look more like small butterflies than flies, and it was these that caught Frankie's attention most. "How much are you selling these down in the pub for?"

Perry told her.

"Get me some more of the butterfly ones and we'll triple that. Couple of dozen ought to do it. Could you make them on a safety pin instead of a hook? I'm thinking there'd be demand for them as jewellery. Brooches might do."

"Priscilla said as much. I'll see what I can get together," he said.

"Great. The more colourful the better. They'll go well with the tropical plants." She went off towards the hothouse and Perry got on with his tasks. Watering, weeding, shovelling. The sun burned down and he was quite content. Talking to Dilys had taken a load off his mind.

The murder case was dragging on without charges. The papers were desperate for an update. "Dead Man's Widow

Questioned Over Murder" "Brewery Killing: Mystery Remains".

The news eventually gave way to other topics, with reporters having milked every employee and ex-employee of the brewery for all they could get. Perry did notice that they didn't seem to have tracked down the Grover fellow. Or maybe they had done, but he'd had nothing to offer.

The merry widow, as Dilys had started referring to Sybil Stanton, was causing Martin's uncle no end of woe badgering him over probate.

Thanks to Ray mentioning her situation to Martin, Dilys had managed to replace her morning at the Stantons' house with working for Harcourt Solicitors. So she had her ear to the ground once again and relayed everything back to the regulars in the Boatswain at the earliest opportunity.

"Always in there, she is. Wasn't at all pleased to see me, I can tell you. Had quite a funny start the first time, then pursed her lips in the way that she does." Dilys gave an impression.

Martin tried not to laugh, feeling he should maintain some professionalism. The Dilys situation was awkward and he had some regrets at having recommended her to his uncle.

She might be useful one day, though, in the same way Perry was. People never took much notice of a cleaner so they saw and heard a lot more than they should.

"Takes a while, doesn't it, to get the money from a will?" Priscilla asked Martin. She was still angling for him but Perry had noticed he never took the bait.

"A good couple of months, and that's if everything's straightforward."

"I bet once she's got it, she'll be off overseas where they can't catch up with her," Priscilla said.

Martin said nothing though he considered that it wasn't beyond the realms of possibility. It also wasn't going to be a very straightforward probate. Foolish Arthur Stanton hadn't made a new will on marriage, and now Sybil was trying to make a claim on joint ownership of the home and the business, aiming to cut Rose Stanton out of as much of her share of the estate as possible.

Unless someone did Sybil in - and much of the time Martin and his uncle privately found themselves wishing someone would - Rose might be left with a fraction of what she should have received.

Strictly speaking the child's problems weren't his concern. The court had already appointed her a solicitor. For now there was a residence order for her to stay in the family home with Sybil but Martin doubted the stepmother planned to look after her long term. She had never made any moves towards adopting her. There had been some mention of cousins of Arthur that "might want the girl" but that was all he knew.

The merry widow, of all people, showed up at Goodlock Nursery the following week.

Perry was there to drop off the fishing flies, or butterflies as they were. He still hadn't decided if he was going to the Festival himself or not. He didn't much care for large crowds but it was a chance to see Priscilla outside her workplace. Even if he wasn't going there with her officially.

He was still weighing it up as he arrived at the nursery. The van wasn't parked outside so Barney must be out again. They worked long hours, those two.

Then he saw Sybil Stanton. She was wearing all the same colour again, this time a mauve shade. She and Frankie were in the shed that served as a shop. Sybil turned around as Perry arrived and looked as though she didn't particularly like what she saw. She showed no signs of recognising him. Stuck up cow.

"I'll be seeing you, then."

Frankie said nothing but looked distracted as the mauve-clad woman departed.

"What did she want?" Perry asked. He put the box of flies on the counter. "Know who she is, don't you?"

Frankie frowned. "Sorry Perry, I'm a bit distracted. Those bromeliads still haven't arrived from Costa Rica and according to the manifest they wired me, the ship they should have been on arrived in port two weeks ago."

Perry knew very little about shipping and couldn't offer any practical help. "That was the Widow Stanton," he said.

"I figured that out."

"She planning on doing up her garden?"

Frankie looked puzzled again. "No. Lilies, she wanted. For the funeral. I think she thought we might have had them cheaper than at a florist. Which we do, but they're not the right kind." She noticed the box for the first time. "Are these the flies? I'll take a look later. I've got to get on the phone about these plants."

Barney pulled up in the van just as Perry was leaving and called out to him. "Just back from Witney. Woman over there wanted six weeping cherries. For a garden the size of a phone box. Still, it pays the bills. Is Frankie in the office?"

"Yes, on the phone about the Costa Rica plants," Perry said.

Barney grimaced. "Not them again. I've had bills of lading coming out of my ears. Let's leave her to it and go for a drink. They're her babies, after all."

Perry didn't mention the visit of Sybil Stanton as they walked along the towpath towards the Boatswain. He was thinking about her, though. Remembering something odd in her expression as she'd glanced over him. He couldn't put his finger on what it was, though.

One thing he did notice was that she looked greedy. No wonder she wanted to skimp on the funeral costs. It was a flaw, greed.

Of course the training was for a reason. You didn't need the equivalent of a PhD in lock picking just for fun. The Company had him do easy jobs at first, easy tasks.

Perry came to realise how interdependent the Company was. Everyone relied on everyone else. It was teamwork. They all had their different jobs and skills, but if one person screwed up, they all fell down.

He himself was never the weakest link. He played his part, opening everything they asked him to. Easily and efficiently. He loved playing with different locks and to start with it felt like a game, almost a treat.

He was about ten years old by this point. As he started to realise the significance of what he was doing, he felt some pride that he was so useful to them.

Once or twice there were slip ups, though not on Perry's part. If they ran into a bolt that couldn't be slipped, they'd jemmy a window. The man who did this was called Emmanuel and he wasn't as good as he should have been.

King John was busy managing things on a wider scale, or he might have picked up on certain problems. The home electronics business prospered, and he had a lucrative interest in a counterfeiting money laundering network as well as a deal with a Lithuanian who contracted out pickpocketing gangs. He was a big man,

King John. The Company was a flourishing organisation with plenty of profitable activities and fruitful partnerships. There were productive negotiations with the Midlands chapter, and the territorial line was observed by both sides.

Eventually Emmanuel let them down. He got greedy and careless. Took on a bank raid for a rival gang. The police got a tip off and a couple of them got caught: Emmanuel among them. He ended up getting 18 months. He had form, which didn't help.

But it was from this point that Perry realised the Company's work was serious business. It wasn't a game and he couldn't afford to slip up.

Also at this time he was starting to consider that he didn't really want to do what he was doing, but he couldn't see a way out.

6

It was a good day for the Midsummer Festival. Hot and dry. It was a colourful affair. Thousands of people flocked through the fields in rainbow clothes, beads, tattoos and piercings. Even in the open air the place reeked of patchouli and cannabis.

Perry wandered around, bought some citronella joss sticks to keep midges away, and manned the stall for Frankie when she went for a break. She managed to sell around half of her plants and all of Perry's fishing flies.

"Are these just for show?" a girl asked, looking over them.

"They're totems," Frankie told her. "Different colours for different chakras."

The girl bought three.

"We should have put an extra zero on the price," Frankie said.

Perry wasn't sure whether he felt glad about earning a few extra quid or bad for the girl paying an already inflated price.

Barney Goodlock had come along too, and Martin and Mary. Mary could only stay a couple of hours because of having to work in the pub. Saturdays were always heaving this time of year, what with the river traffic. Perry looked out for Priscilla though he barely got a glimpse of her.

Mary was trying to decide whether a purple crushed velvet waistcoat would look nice or not.

"It would look better on your brother," Barney said. Damon was supposedly there but no one had seen him. Barney bought a paper bag of mushrooms. "For making tea," the vendor told him, with a nudge and a wink.

Barney took one out and twirled it in his fingers. "They'd better be the right kind."

"You're the horticulturalist," Frankie said. Barney had done a course in horticulture; Frankie was self-taught.

"I can never tell. Bit deadly if you get it wrong."

To Perry they looked much like the mushrooms they used to sell at a fairground he'd once worked at. Skinny little toadstools with thin stems. But he was no expert either.

The five of them got wasted on scrumpy and "bonza brownies" sold by an Australian backpacker on the stall next to Frankie's. They all knew what was in them. But it was midsummer and everyone was content to get carried away.

"I'm in no fit state to pull pints," Mary said. She stood up and then sat down again, giggling.

"I'll walk you back," Barney offered. "Can't have you falling in the canal." He was more sober than the others.

Mary staggered off with him, still laughing.

"Do you get to travel overseas much, in your line of work?" Martin asked Frankie. He had gone full city yokel, lying on his side in designer sunglasses, chewing on a stem of meadow grass.

"Once or twice a year. Mainly to keep suppliers on their toes. It's not much of a holiday, though, one of us always has stay behind and man the shop."

"I can imagine," Martin said. "My uncle gets a locum. Couldn't you do that?"

Frankie was lying on her back, weaving a ribbon between her braids. "We could, but it's a matter of cash. I'd get Perry here to mind it, he knows the ropes, but even you'd want pay, wouldn't you?"

"I suppose so." Perry hadn't given it any thought.

Frankie laughed. "I bet you'd do it anyway, if I only asked you. I won't though. I'm not that much of an exploiter." She sat up. "It's the same for Ray and Mary. You get tied down, running a business. Sometimes I think it would be easier to stay on a wage."

They started a conversation about the most ideal jobs: those that you could work your own hours and not have to commit to regular clients.

"Prostitute, I'd say," Frankie suggested. "Even if you had regular clients you could shift them around a bit."

"If you went on holiday you might lose them, if they went to someone else and preferred it," Martin said.

"Do hookers have locums?" Frankie wondered. She and Martin started calculating how many hours you'd need to work and what you'd have to charge if you wanted to be on the game and earn as much as a doctor.

They weren't really caring what they were saying, Perry thought, just talking for the sake of it. He blamed it on the brownies. People always talked random rubbish when they were high, but you could still have a normal conversation if they were drunk.

He himself was sobering up. He took another swig of the scrumpy but there wasn't much left.

Then that evening they all got pissed again in the Boatswain. You couldn't hold a conversation above the noise of the band that Ray had booked so everyone drank instead. The bar staff were all rushed off their feet.

As Ray called last orders, Mary decided to have a lock-in as she was in a party spirit. "Something about midsummer, it makes me want to stay up all night and dance," she said. Not that there was any dancing at the Boatswain in the normal course of events.

Perry thought that Mary looked a bit giddy. She was probably still high from earlier in the day, he reasoned. It took longer to wear off with some people.

When the band had packed up, and a few people had drifted off, the doors were locked. It was still pretty crowded as no one wanted to go home so early on a Saturday night. The lock-in meant Mary and Ray could now keep the pub open a while longer under the licensing laws, so long as no one else was admitted through the door. All the customers were supposed to have put money behind the bar before the official closing time at eleven o'clock. But in practice people just paid as and when, and Ray ran it all through the till the next day.

"It's got a nice, exclusive feeling, a lock in," Dilys Jones said. She hadn't been at the festival but she'd made her way down to the pub later on. She drank there because she got a small discount as a bonus to her cleaning work.

"Like being a member of a private club?" Martin asked.

"You'd know all about that." Dilys considered that all university students spent most of their time haring around the city on bicycles, clad in white tie, and getting drunk on champagne at balls and banquets.

"You ought to have come to the festival earlier, Dill," Mary said. "There was a good crowd."

Dilys grimaced. "You won't catch me there. All those mad hags selling crystals and tat."

"Frankie's plants did alright though. Sold most of them, didn't you?"

Frankie was fiddling with the end of one of her braids. The bead had come off and she was trying to reattach it. "We did alright. Got rid of a load of kalanchoes that were slow to shift at the nursery."

"Are they tropical then? You can get them over here easy. I wouldn't have thought you needed to import them," Mary said.

"Only some varieties," Frankie explained. "These were some rarer ones."

Dilys went off to the bathroom and the conversation moved on from plants.

Barney said he was peckish. "What food have you got, Mary?"

It was all packets. Crisps, pork scratchings, cashews, peanuts.

"Salted or dry roasted?" Barney asked. Both, he was told. He got Mary to bring out the roasted ones. Dilys related a tragic tale about a girl who died when kissing her boyfriend after he'd eaten peanut butter.

"He'd eaten it hours before. There was nothing detectable left. Just the tiniest, tiniest trace that they couldn't pick up on. But enough to kill her."

"Be a good way to murder someone," Martin said.

Mary shivered. "You two are morbid. I'll bring out the cashews next time."

It seemed as though they were all sitting around drinking for hours. What they talked about was anyone's guess. Perry was so plastered by the time he staggered home that he could barely see straight.

"For God's sake don't go falling in the canal," Mary called after him. "Perhaps you'd better see him back, Dill."

"You'll be fine, won't you, Perry?" Dilys shouted.

Too far gone to respond verbally, Perry raised a hand as he walked away from them. He'd pay for it in the morning but he wasn't lucid enough to think about that now.

Midsummer, the solstice, the longest day. It would get darker from here on, though they wouldn't notice it for a while.

Darkness was a friend. It was a welcome cover for the Company's activities. You had to be able to get by in the dark and do all that you needed to do.

Perry learnt quickly. Faster than Jake even, and Jake was the golden boy. Perry hero-worshipped him.

Jake had been picking pockets since he was a small kid. He'd barely been to school, his attendance made Perry look like a scholar. Jake's mother was a "tart", Black Bessie had once told Perry. Bessie hadn't liked her.

"Stab you in the back soon as look at you," she said.

Like Perry, Jake had no idea who his father was.

"Some punter," he'd once said but after that they never spoke of it.

Jake could brush past a woman in the street, slit the fabric of her bag, have her purse up his sleeve and be out of sight in seconds. Perry was hugely impressed but Jake advised him to stick to his locks. "I'm not saying you couldn't learn, but there's no point to it. Chances are you might only come away with a handful of coppers and a library ticket. It's a big risk for just that."

7

It had gone completely dark for Sybil Stanton, née Sybil Smythe.

One bullet: one life. Gone forever.

"Widow Shot Dead With Same Gun." "Contract Killing Suspect in Brewery Case". "Police Say Still No Leads on Brewery Murders".

Sybil's body had been found on the towpath half a mile from the Boatswain, shot cleanly through the back of the head at close range. The nearest landmark was Perry's mooring.

After a big night, Perry was in no fit state when the police came knocking on Sunday morning. A jogger had found the body, hidden by the shadow of a bush until dawn. Perry figured he must have walked straight past it on the way home. Though he'd been so blind drunk he wouldn't have noticed a dozen or more bodies strewn about the place.

The police were convinced Perry must have at least heard something but he managed to explain he'd been out. "I was in the Boatswain."

"Until what time?"

Men's wallets were richer pickings than women's purses but even then Jake said it was more trouble than it was worth nowadays.

"When I was a kid everyone carried cash. Now it's all cards, and that's a different line of business entirely."

Perry wasn't sure. He'd had so much to drink he couldn't remember looking at the time. "They had a lock-in."

The police went to the pub next where they took statements from Mary and Ray. "Yes, we'd have been in a lock-in by that time," Mary confirmed. "No one came in or out after eleven that I remember. You can check with the other staff when they come in."

The police couldn't wait for that, so Mary handed out names and addresses.

The facts were straightforward enough. The fatal shooting had taken place at around half past eleven.

There were a half a dozen or so witnesses, several of them canal folk, who claimed they'd heard the shot. A couple of others claimed to have heard a loud bang forty minutes earlier, but the detectives figured this must have been a car backfiring. Later medical evidence also put the time of death between ten o'clock Saturday and two o'clock Sunday.

Perry made his way to the pub where Mary cooked him breakfast. He could hardly face bacon and eggs but Mary told him to get it down him. "It'll do you a power of good."

They were all hungover. And now shell-shocked from the latest revelations.

"There were quite a few people leaving here around eleven," Mary said. "You'd think a load of them might have walked that way and seen something."

It wasn't really on the way to anything except his boat, Perry thought. But he didn't say anything.

"Or one of them might have done it," Ray pointed out. "Maybe that's why they chose that time, with so many possible suspects."

"If they were holiday boaters they might be long gone by now," Mary said.

The police had their work cut out, that was for sure.

Word soon spread and all the usual people trickled back to the Boatswain by evening, swapping stories. There was police tape all down past the canal, where scenes-of-crime officers had been active most of the day. The body was long gone in an ambulance to the morgue.

"Back with her husband," Dilys said. "Bet she wasn't bargaining on that."

Dilys was convinced that Sybil Stanton had arranged for Arthur to be shot. "She hired someone, and then gypped on the payment, and then he did her in." Dilys wouldn't precisely reveal why she thought this. "I've got my reasons," she said darkly.

"You ought to be careful then, Dilys," Ray said. He was in a good mood, the murders were turning out to be excellent business for him. Crowds of locals and tourists flocked to visit the crime scene, people were ghoulish like that, and they inevitably stopped by the Boatswain for a tipple and to dig out any extra gossip. Sunday evenings were usually on the quieter side but it was very busy that night.

"Careful? No one's after me." Dilys was scornful.

"They might be, if that tongue of yours keeps wagging."

Mary came over, picking up used ashtrays and putting empty ones down. Dilys chain smoked, and Ray enjoyed a crafty one when Mary wasn't looking. He was supposed to have given up. Perry had avoided ever getting into the habit. "You solved the murder yet, then?" Mary asked them.

"Dilys reckons she has," Ray said. "I reckon she's got no more clue than any of us." He went back to the bar.

Martin had been quieter, still in a kind of professional limbo since Sybil had been his uncle's client. Her death made everything even more complex.

"I wonder who all that money she was after goes to now." Dilys drew another cigarette out and flicked her lighter against it.

"Less than thirty days, so likely the kid or the Crown," Martin said.

Priscilla was hovering near, collecting glasses. "What's that about thirty days?"

Martin explained. "To inherit, you have to survive the deceased by thirty days. If you die right after them, it all goes to the next person in line."

"Maybe that person did her in, then."

"Given that person is a twelve-year-old girl, it's unlikely," Martin said.

Dilys started. "The kid! I'd forgotten her. Who'll be minding her? There's no one else in that house, is there?"

No one had any idea. Dilys was the only one properly acquainted with the family.

"Social services will have it covered," Martin said.

Perry didn't react but he immediately felt troubled.

"She'll be scared," Dilys said. "And all alone. I know she couldn't stand the stepmother, but still."

"Should we go over there, do you think?" Mary asked her.

Dilys stubbed out her cigarette. "Might be an idea. There aren't any relatives here, so far as I know."

There weren't many relatives around for Sybil either. The newspapers managed to put together a scant biography. She had been born forty-four years ago as Sybil Enid Smythe, the daughter and only child of Cyril Smythe, a clerk in a tea company, and Maureen Smythe née Shaw, who had taught piano part-time. Both Cyril and Maureen Smythe were long dead.

Sybil had left school with some thought of becoming a concert pianist, though a lack of talent and opportunity soon saw this dream fizzle out. She had then worked a number of little jobs while living at home, presumably waiting for marriage. It didn't arrive. After her parents died she had moved to a small cottage, eking out a living teaching a bit of piano herself and occasionally playing for hire. She hadn't been very popular in the village where she had lived, with neighbours describing her as prim and snobbish.

"Thought she was above everyone else," was the verdict.

She had met Arthur Stanton while playing at an event for Brewery staff and their wives. When one of the brewers took over the keys to play a more raucous melody, the widowed Arthur found himself asking the trim, smartly dressed lady pianist for a turn on the dance floor.

He had been taken with her ladylike airs, thinking she might do as a stepmother to Rose. Within three months they were married. Unfortunately the new bride and the stepdaughter had disliked each other on sight. Sybil, having had no children of her own was not interested in anyone else's, and was counting the years until she'd finally be rid of the girl.

Instead, she was got rid of first.

Sybil had had one real friend and companion, a mousy, nervous little woman called Miss Sparks. The police tried to get what they could out of Miss Sparks, to see if there were any clues to Sybil Smythe's demise in her private affairs. Miss Sparks was a hopelessly nervous and stupid interviewee, constantly twittering on about "poor, dear Sybil, such a loss!" and how she herself had no notion of business or what went on behind the scenes at the Brewery. The police had disclosed some of this to Martin's uncle, since he had been acting for the late widow.

Miss Sparks was, if nothing else, convinced that Sybil's murder must be related to her husband's business. The police were inclined to think the same. Sybil had no money, had lived a quiet and apparently law abiding life, and had no close associates other than her husband and Miss Sparks.

Among the regulars at the Boatswain, Dilys was the only one who had ever had anything to do with her. Sybil had not, to anyone's knowledge, ever entered the pub.

What she was doing near the canal at midnight, and why she had been shot, remained a mystery.

Murder was not part of the Company's modus operandi. Even violence was to be avoided. There might be times, King John reasoned, when someone deserved a good drubbing. But in the regular course of events it was a distraction and a waste of energy.

No one ever really applied concepts of right and wrong to the Company's activities. They did stuff that the police didn't want them to do, that was all Perry knew. You had to do your job, and get out before the coppers came.

"Scuffers" King John called them. They all knew about him but could never get anything on him. Once in a while they'd try to pressure another Company member into giving information, but anyone privy to King John's business was also loyal to the grave. For it would be the grave, if they grassed. So Jake warned Perry anyway.

There were few tears shed over the loss of Emmanuel. King John had a new recruit lined up almost immediately, who was a "much surer pair of hands", as he put it.

The Company was mainly doing over warehouses in those days, Perry at least. Commercial premises involved more work for him. If it was a house he could sort out the front door or back door lock and then scarper if he wished. With a warehouse he might be needed for interior doors, drawers and cabinets.

It was amazing the amount of tip offs that the Company got. Half the industrial work came through insiders, bent employees who'd leave a padlock off, tip King John the wink and take a cut later on.

Everyone was on the take so how was Perry even to get a sense that it was wrong? He simply understood that it was risky. That he had to be quick and careful, and learn to slip away as King John did. Jake was good at melting into crowds, and Perry learnt from him.

8

Later that evening Perry walked back along the canal, enjoying the heavier scents of nature sweetened up by the earlier heat. Mown grass and hay, wayside flowers, the still waters of the canal.

He skirted around the area cordonned off by the police. No one was guarding it. They'd be lucky if kids hadn't vandalised it by morning. Still, they probably had all they needed by now.

When he approached the Emerald he could see a dark mass on the deck by the door. A figure, huddled over. A small figure.

Even before he was close enough to see, Perry guessed by some instinct who it was.

He kept his voice low. "Rosie Stanton, what are you doing here?"

The figure looked up at him. He could see a pale face and the shine of eyes. She didn't say anything.

Perry tried again. "Does anyone know you're here?"

"Didn't have anywhere else to go. They were going to put me in care." Rose's voice wobbled on these last words.

"I shouldn't think they'd do that, so quickly. Don't you have a friend you could stay with?"

Again she didn't answer and he sighed, going past her to open the door.

"You use a key for your door then?"

"Can't lock it without one."

She hadn't thought of that. "They said you can open them with your eyes closed."

"Doesn't make much difference either way. You can't see inside a lock, can you?" But he wasn't going to be distracted by the subject. Someone would be looking for the kid and Perry needed to let them know where she was. He'd have to call the police, or get Mary to.

"How long have you been here, Rosie?"

"I don't know. First I went round Dilys's but she wasn't there." Dilys's place was to the north of the city. The kid must have walked a fair way. "Then I came here."

"You'll have to go back, there'll be people worried about you. They'll be looking for you."

Rose was defiant. "No one's worried about me. And I'm not going back."

"You can't stay out here all night. You come along to the pub with me now. We can use the phone there," Perry said.

The head shot up. "If you make me go I'll jump in the canal, I swear I will."

Perry was at a loss. "I'll go myself then. I'll see if I can find Dilys and bring her back with me."

"You'll bring the police back."

He had honestly no intention of doing so. "I promise you, Rosie, I'll just get Dilys." Or Mary, if Dilys wasn't there.

"I don't believe you!"

She was overwrought, he could hear it in her voice. God knew she'd been through enough. Losing her father, stuck with a stepmother who loathed her, then about to lose her home. She'd had as much as she could take, and she was only a kid.

"How about I make us some tea and then you have a think about going back?" It would buy them both some time. Once the girl calmed down she might see reason.

Rose didn't respond for a few moments. She was thinking it over. He saw the glare on her face ease. "Okay. I won't change my mind though. I'm never, ever going back."

She followed him into the cabin where he lit the battery lamp and went to turn on the gas stove to boil the kettle. Rose was looking around, curious about everything. "Don't you have electricity?" she asked.

"No real need." He could have put in a generator to run a fridge, but they were noisy and he had no particular interest in a television. Gas cylinders were easy to replace and heated water quickly. He often didn't bother switching the immersion heater on in summer, showering in cold water instead.

While the kettle boiled Perry went back outside and hauled up a container on the end of a rope. Rose watched him. "What's that?"

"Keeps things cooler in summer." He unscrewed the lid, which was watertight, and took out a bottle of milk.

"Wouldn't a fridge be easier?" Rose asked.

"No point, just for me. Besides, they hum all night."

When the water was ready he poured it onto tea bags in two mugs, then topped them up with milk. He offered her sugar and she took two spoonfuls. He stirred one in his own mug.

Rose sipped it. "It tastes like normal tea," she said.

"It is normal tea."

"I thought it might be different, on a boat."

Perry was hungry and figured she must be too, so he opened up a can of soup and tipped it into a pan, turning up the gas. He felt her eyes on his every move.

"Don't you have a campfire?"

He half laughed at this. "It's a boat, Rosie, not a tent." She seemed disappointed. He tried to explain. "I live here all year round, see. It's not like a camping trip."

"Wish I lived on a boat. I'd move it about though and see different places."

It got Perry wondering why he stayed put for so long. Saving up for the engine was one issue, but he knew in some ways it was an excuse. He should get on the move again soon. Then there wouldn't be complications like this kid hanging around.

There were other ties too. He'd got some good, regular work here. Friends, even.

Perry poured the soup into the mugs they'd finished drinking the tea from, after quickly rinsing them. The bread he had was going stale but it was fine toasted. He took the mugs outside for them to drink on the deck because he wanted to get her outside the boat. After this he was walking her back to the pub.

But he didn't reckon on Rose.

If the kid had been obstinate before, she was immovable now. "I'm not going anywhere. I'm staying here."

"You can't stay here. It's not..." Perry groped for the right words. "I can't be responsible for a kid. It wouldn't be allowed."

Rose looked scornful. "I don't need looking after. I'm not a little child." She sounded even younger when she said this.

Perry was starting to give in. "You can doss down here one night, and that's it. Tomorrow you go back. And I will fetch the police if you don't, and I don't care if you do jump in the canal." He was fairly sure it was an empty threat.

She was elated. She hadn't really expected him to yield. "Where do I sleep?"

"I'll show you." He led her back inside to the bunk area. Only his bunk was made up, and he didn't have much in the way of blankets for a second person. It got him thinking that if he did ever get Priscilla or another woman in here, he might have to make better arrangements.

He put most of his blankets on the spare bunk then fetched down an old sleeping bag from a cabinet above. He rolled up a towel for a pillow. "That's the best I can do."

"It's great." She was all aglow, relieved and grateful. It moved him. Likely she hadn't been shown much kindness since her father died. She was just in the way and she knew it.

They lay there in the darkness, Perry wondering what kind of a mess it was all going to be the next day. If they'd put out a search for her, he might be in bad trouble for harbouring her. He wasn't sure if it mightn't count as kidnapping. Martin would know, or his uncle. That was absolutely the last thing he wanted, trouble with the law again.

"Perry?" A small, hesitant voice in the darkness.

"Go to sleep, Rosie."

"I didn't kill her. I know I wanted to, but I didn't do it. Honest."

Was that what this was all about? Silly kid, no wonder she had run away. "I know you didn't. No one's thinking you did it, Rosie. They're looking for some older fellow with a gun."

"You know that box of hers?"

He remembered the box.

"It's gone."

There was silence again.

"Perry?"

"What now?"

"If they can't find out who killed my dad, will you find out for me?"

"They'll find him. But don't you think about that now. They've got it all in hand," Perry said.

"Promise me?"

It wasn't a promise he could keep even if he intended, but words were cheap. "I promise." As he said it, he hoped he hadn't committed to something he might be called on to do.

After a few moments, Rose said: "I wish I could live here always."

Perry was about to tell her to be quiet again when he realised she had fallen asleep. He lay awake for hours, listening to her breathing, wondering how the hell he had got into this mess and how he was going to get out of it.

It was a mark you got, King John said, once you'd been inside. Like a taint. You could always tell. So the wise gentleman, he instructed the young Perry, made sure to avoid accepting an invitation to Her Majesty's Pleasure at all costs. Keep out of trouble. Don't take unnecessary risks.

Jake the Flick was nodding during this lesson. He'd once escaped with a suspended sentence after getting caught in a fight. Since then he'd learnt more caution: he kept his blade sharp and his nose clean these days.

"So you see, Beck my lad, you don't take any chances you don't need to. It's not about heroes, this game. It's about doing your work in a business-like fashion," King John proclaimed.

King John liked to talk in business terms as it lent legitimacy to the Company's operations. He also determined what activities the Company engaged in, and when. Banks were out, too high risk with all the electronics security and cameras these days. He was looking into recruiting some specialists in that area but for now, banks and building societies were off the cards. So was what he called "the Bristol", the trade in drugs between Bristol and Birmingham. "Best left to the Jamaicans," was all he had to say about that.

He introduced Perry to other areas of the business. Perry soon learnt, after King John cuffed him around the ear for greeting someone in the street, that there were people - pawnbrokers, antiques dealers and other select resellers - whom you were supposed to pretend not to know. Even if you'd been with them in the back room of their shop a day earlier.

Wheeling and dealing behind the scenes: perfect strangers if you saw them anywhere else.

9

Perry woke before Rose the next morning. He'd slept in later than he usually did, after a troubled night.

The kid was still sleeping so he washed up the soup mugs from the previous evening and put the kettle on for tea. He sat out on the deck, warming his hands on the mug while he drank from it. It was fresh that morning, a nip in the air. Grey overcast skies, bright but damp.

Monday morning, the start of a new week. All the summer stretching ahead of him. It was a good place to be in the world.

Yet his sense of well-being was eroded as he saw a stray bit of police tape blowing along the towpath. There was a taint on the season. If he moved upriver, found another mooring, would he be able to shake it off?

He stretched, cracking out the sleep from his muscles. There was a tree nearby with a branch where he did a few chin-ups. It was a legacy of the days with Jake. "If you can haul yourself up, you can always get over a wall and get away," Jake had told him.

Perry didn't have much cause for escaping blind alleys these days. But he kept up the exercise partly in tribute to Jake.

He realised he was now about the same age that Jake had been when he got shot. It was a sobering thought.

Making his way back into the cabin he tried to rouse the girl. "Rose," he said. "Rosie". He didn't know if he should shake her. In detention she'd have had a bucket of water on her by now.

But she opened her eyes of her own accord, sleepy and wary, forgetting for a moment where she was.

"We've got to get going, Rosie."

She acquiesced. He sensed a new attitude in her this morning. He had won her trust.

They trekked along the towpath to the Boatswain together without talking. Perry guessed that Rose was worried about having run away. It was bad enough if she'd been missed and people would be angry with her. It was even worse if no one had missed her.

They reached the pub. Dilys cleaned on Monday mornings which was a fortunate thing. There she was in her scarf and overalls, just arriving in the car park as Perry and Rose got there.

"Rose Stanton. What are you doing here?" There was relief and concern on Dilys's face. "Had the police call me up last night, I did. Where've you been?"

She looked at Perry. "We had a bit of a stowaway situation," he told her.

"You silly kid. Come here." Dilys put her arms out and Rose ran into them, breaking into sobs. Perry felt awkward. He had no idea what to do around a crying girl. Best let Dilys handle it.

"I'll be in the pub." He left them there, Dilys chiding Rose for giving everyone a scare.

"Thought you'd been abducted, we did. Or been run over. They called all the hospitals."

Inside Perry got a ticking off from Mary. "Could have got yourself mixed up in all sorts of trouble. Next time you bring her straight back."

"She was threatening all sorts," Perry explained. "I've got no idea why she showed up in the first place. I only saw her once before."

"It's your boat. It's exciting to a kid, that. Like an adventure."

Mary rang up the police for Perry. "Local bloke found the kid on his boat and brought her back. She's here at the Boatswain with us. That's the one, down by the canal past Goodlocks'. Yes, I'll keep her here, she'll be quite safe."

A female officer arrived with a social worker within the hour. Rose scowled when she saw them. They'd got the impression that she had broken into the boat by herself and that Perry had been out all night and only found her in the morning. Rose was smart enough not to correct them, and Perry felt relief that he was off the hook for harbouring a runaway.

There was a fuss when Rose wouldn't go with them. "I'm not going to a kids' home. I'll run away again." She tilted up her chin, looking both defiant and pathetic. Her eyes glittered and her hands were clenched. Perry could see that she was trying not to cry and he felt bad for her. She wasn't his problem though.

"We'll get the paperwork done, have you with a nice family by tonight," the social worker said.

"I won't go. I'm staying with Dilys."

Dilys looked sorry. "I can't take you, love. I've only got the one room and there's evening shifts. You know I would if I could."

"Then I'm staying here. I'll camp."

"You can't camp by yourself. You're not old enough."

"I've got my own house. I'll stay there."

The social worker looked weary. "Like I said, we can't let you stay anywhere alone without a grown-up. We're trying to get hold of your auntie in Yorkshire for you. It'll just be for a few days." She looked back to Perry and Mary. "Seems they're overseas right now."

Rose was close to a meltdown.

Mary broke in. "We've got a spare room here. It's not in much of a state, full of boxes and that, but I can clear it out. We can put her up for a couple of days."

Hope flared in Rose's eyes. "I want to stay with Mary."

The social worker and police officer exchanged a glance. "We'll see what can be done," the social worker said. "We might get an emergency order through. Only temporary though, we still have to find you somewhere permanent, Rose. You want your own bedroom don't you? All your own things?"

Rose didn't respond. She clung to Dilys and looked mutinous.

"I'll make a call back to the agency and have a check round here. You'll have to come down and sign some things," the social worker said. "She should be at school, too. Term's nearly out I suppose."

It was all arranged. Rose and Mary had to go with them to get the papers signed. Dilys got stuck into her cleaning.

Perry felt like a spare wheel so he wandered back out again and down to the canal.

There was to be no peace for the wicked. Sitting on his deck again, tying a fly, Perry was interrupted by more unwelcome visitors.

King John Lochinvar stood there once again, shaking his head.

"What you fiddling with that rubbish for? You taken up angling?"

Old Owen was with him again, and a slack-jawed bloke a couple of years younger than Perry. King John made the introductions.

"This is the boy Joe. This is Perry Beck, Joe. The one as I was telling you of."

"Arr," said Joe. His mouth hung open.

What had happened to the Company, that King John was reduced to taking on recruits like this? Perry didn't like to ask about the Witney job.

"Bessie sends her regards. And the rest of the family. It's been some years, hasn't it?"

It had. "I trust they're all fine," Perry said.

"Ah, well now. That's partly as why I've stopped by. Perhaps we might go for a drop again, have a long catch up? For old times' sake."

Perry did not want this. Being seen with them once in the White Stag was enough. "I've got some beers here." There wasn't much room on the deck for all four of them, but they managed to perch around the edge. Perry retrieved the cans from his underwater store and handed them around. Old Owen had to crack the boy Joe's open for him after he struggled with the ring pull.

King John took a deep draught and then sat back, holding his beer on his broad thigh. "It's like this, see," he began, and the tale of woe began.

Times had grown lean for the Company over the past few years. Since the loss of Jake and the authorities dispersing most of them, they'd never quite got the momentum back. Perry knew that King John had once been a major figure, a literal kingpin, as slippery as he was.

They'd had some key people desert for other associations. Black Bessie, so adept as a forger, saw less demand for her talents now cheques were going by the wayside. Worse, the Midlands chapter had edged in to Banbury and some fighting had broken out among their men and King John's men.

"Waste of resources, I call it," King John said. "Used to be that there was plenty for all." He'd even moved in to the exotics, he told Perry, which meant drugs. Arrests on the Bristol to Birmingham route had opened up some opportunities for others. "Got a little operation going down Swindon way. Wholesale."

He drained the can and slapped it down on the deck. "What we need is some new blood, and the best of the old. Would we could get Jake back, God rest his soul..."

"...God rest his soul," echoed Old Owen, crossing himself.

"But that's not possible. But there's you, Perry, and there's Davy Prout, and Morgan the Organ. Gone Cardiff way, but we'll get him back."

Perry interrupted him. "Like you said, John, it's been some years. I'm in other lines of work now."

King John picked up one of the flies, nearly spearing his finger. "These frippery little things? Can't imagine you get more than few bob for these, Beck."

"They're a hobby. It's other things I do. Got some labouring work, it's a good situation."

"Afraid to rock the boat? The narrowboat?" King John roared with laughter at his own joke and the boy Joe gave a gormless grin.

"Something like that," Perry said.

King John was used to getting his way but he could be patient about reeling them in. "You think on what I've said. Easier work, more money. Career opportunities too, that's what all the kids want these days, isn't it? There's the Guild, don't forget."

The Guild. The shadowy organisation that overarched all the various Companies across the land. King John held some role within it, as did all his counterparts.

Perry dared to ask: "What happened with that job in Witney?"

A cloud fell over King John's ruddy face. "Wasn't all it was cracked up to be, that job. We took a pass on that one. But we'll say no more about that, because it pains Old Owen and myself to think of."

Perry remembered Davy Prout. He'd been a kind of deputy for King John in the early days, but there'd been a falling out and he'd dropped out of sight for a while.

He'd slunk back eventually but had never regained quite the same favour. A professional burglar since way back, Davy had a self-seeking streak which didn't sit well with the Company.

Burgling was a win-win business, he claimed. "No one gets harmed. They've all got insurance, see? We get a bit of merchandise and the kiddies who live there get a nice new telly. Everybody's happy."

Davy meticulously re-burgled every house three months later. By this time the insurance money would have paid for a fresh set of shiny new electronics.

Business was booming.

10

If it wasn't enough taking on Rose and dealing with all that involved, Mary and Ray were having headaches that week with the pub. A firm that was supposed to have come in during the week to redo the beer dispensing system had cancelled, wanting to reschedule for Saturday.

"We can't close up then, it's our busiest lunchtime," Mary said.

Ray took it in his stride. "There's not a lot we can do. It's got to be done some time. Otherwise they say they can't fit us in for over a month. The current pipes and pumps have had it." He went off to the cellar, leaving Mary at the bar with Perry and Dilys.

Since they had little choice, Mary decided they'd have to make the best of it. "It's Ray's birthday next week. We'll have a barbecue party for him, as the forecast's fine. Just staff and a few friends and regulars. It's time we had something to take us away from all this nasty business. Then once they've finished up inside we'll open up for the evening crowd."

Dilys was on board and Perry thought it was a fine idea. Barney and Frankie had a Saturday girl who could mind the till in the nursery shop for them, so they were good to drop by for a couple of hours. Priscilla made a point of inviting Martin when he next came in. Ray asked a couple of the beer-bellied bar bores he was mates with. It was turning out to be quite a crowd.

Mary was right that a distraction would be healthy. Sybil Stanton's murder hung over the place like a grey cloud. It had taken place so close by and the police still seemed to have no leads on the culprit. People had started to give up talking about it but they still thought about it.

Dilys showed up at the barbecue with a cake she'd made for Ray. It had sunk in the middle, she explained, so she'd tried to fill the depression with cream. Then this had sunk too.

"Not to worry," she said to Perry who had just arrived there himself. "Ray doesn't have much of a sweet tooth. Men don't, do they?"

Perry had never really hankered for sugar after a season spent working on fairgrounds, living off leftover candy floss, broken toffee apples and burgers as he had done. He supposed it might be so.

It had dawned grey and overcast but the sun was burning off the grizzle by late morning and it was warming up. Priscilla showed up in white jeans and a tank top and made a beeline for Martin.

"How are they going?" Barney asked Ray, referring to the men who were supposed to be fixing the new dispensing system.

"Claim they'll have it up and running in time. Don't hold your breath," Ray said. He was turning over some burgers.

One of the regulars, Ray's mates, had already necked down a few bottled drinks. "Are we alright to slip in and use the facilities?" he asked Mary. "Not switched off the plumbing have they?"

"Not so far as I know," Mary told him. "You'd better ask them."

He went off and Mary sat down next to Frankie, who was sitting on a reclining deckchair with a glass of wine. Rose was scoffing packets of crisps nearby. "You're supposed to put those in the bowl and hand them round, Rose." Rose opened a new packet and tipped it in the bowl, and handed it to Mary who handed it to Frankie.

"Thanks Mary. This is the life." Frankie lay back and tilted her face towards the sun. She was wearing large round sunglasses.

"It would be, if we didn't have to open up in a couple of hours," Mary said. "Be nice to be rich and do this all year round."

"Not here though," Frankie said. "You don't get days like this all year round in England. You'd have go somewhere warm."

"Marbella?" Mary suggested.

"They have winters. You'd need somewhere tropical. I've always fancied Ecuador."

Barney overheard. "Wouldn't be much of a market for your tropical plants over there. We'd have to start importing English roses."

Frankie grimaced. "I wouldn't be running a nursery over there. Far too much work in that heat."

"You going on holiday anywhere then?" Mary asked.

"Can't afford to, with the nursery's peak season being summer. If we're not bankrupt by Christmas we'll go away then," Barney said. "How about you?"

"Same deal, except we're even busier at Christmas. We might get Ray's brother in to run the place for a week before the festive season starts. Don't know where we'll go at that time of year."

"You might have Damon run it for you," Dilys says. "He must know the ropes by now."

No one said anything. Damon was lying by himself on a picnic rug a short distance away, apparently asleep.

"He was out all night," Mary said, as if to excuse him.

Dilys took a crisp and screwed her face up. "Are these prawn cocktail, Rose? Haven't you got any salt and vinegar?"

"I saved those for Perry," Rose said. "He likes those best." She handed him the last packet of salt and vinegar.

Perry was surprised and embarrassed that Rose would have noticed which flavour he liked. He didn't want to take the crisps if Dilys wanted them, and he'd have been content with any flavour. But to hand them straight over to Dilys would be a snub to Rose. "Thanks Rosie," he said. "How about I share some with Dilys?"

Dilys was telling them about her plans to get away. "I thought I'd try housesitting," she said. "Of course you're not likely to end up by the sea, since that's where they're all going to. But you get to stay in a big house in another part of the country. If you fix it up privately and there are pets to look after, you can even get a bit of cash on top."

It sounded alright to Perry. He suspected they would do background checks however, which would rule him out.

"Should we put candles on this cake then, Dilys?" Mary asked.

"You can, but I didn't bring any."

"Since it's outside it won't really show the flames anyway, will it? We'll just cut it as it is. You going to do the honours, Ray?"

Ray, still wielding a pair of tongs, said they'd need a clean knife. "This one's all over sausage grease."

Mary said there would be one in the kitchen. Frankie offered to get it. "I could do with the loo. I'll fetch it on my way out." Getting up from her deckchair she was replaced by Barney who had just come back from taking a leak himself.

The barbecue stretched on into the early afternoon. The workmen had finally packed up and the beer was running again through the new system. but nobody could be bothered to move and open up. A lethargy had descended, with the heat, food and alcohol making people lazy. Perry lost track of the time since the sun stayed high in the sky for so long at this time of year.

"We should make a move," Mary said a couple of times, but never did.

"You ought to do this more often," Dilys said. "Put it on for the customers."

Ray shook his head. "Too much of a business. You need the full outdoor catering rig, and you've got all the extra health and safety headaches. Besides, you only get a few days like this a year. It's not worth the investment."

There was a sudden cry from over by the table near the barbecue.

The remains of the cake had attracted wasps and Rose had been stung on the arm. Mary rushed over to her to take a look. "It's vinegar you'll want to put on that, if it's a wasp," Dilys called.

"It really hurts." Rose was near to crying.

"We'll go in and try the vinegar. We can put Savlon on it if that will help," Mary said and took Rose indoors.

Dilys watched them go. "It's not her year, is it? Poor kid. She's been such a tough little thing over everything, or she's tried to be. We were in the street the other day when a car backfired, it sounded just like a gun shot. She was absolutely terrified. She was there when her father got shot, I suppose she must have heard it. It stays with you, something like that."

Darkness descended when Perry was fourteen. They'd done a job and everything had gone against them. There'd been a mix up. There was a rival group that had got hold of guns. So the police, thinking it was the other lot doing over the warehouse, came armed.

It had been a blur then as it was a blur now.

A scuffle. A stand-off. Jake got shot.

The rest of them - except for King John who'd melted away from the scene, Perry never knew how - got arrested.

Jake didn't make it.

Perry remembered the noise. How loud it was, how sharp, how quick.

Everything over in that fraction of time. One single moment.

Perry ended up with eighteen months in juvenile detention. The legal aid brief was useless and never even made an effort. The judge was a vindictive old beak who was sick of young offenders and saw his chance to make an example of someone.

Every exacerbating factor was weighted in to the penalty. A significant degree of planning. Member of a group or gang. Weapon present on entry - Perry had a penknife in his pocket. It wasn't even a flick knife. Equipped for burglary - his wires. He didn't even carry proper tools because King John had told him the police couldn't do you for just carrying a few bits of wire. They didn't count as tools, King John said.

But King John wasn't a lawyer and he was wrong.

Perry was numb throughout the proceedings. All he could think of was that Jake was dead. He never got to see the body and no one ever told him whether there was a funeral or not.

No one came to his trial. They were mostly banged up as well, except for King John, so it wasn't surprising.

11

Having rejected the Company's offer, Perry found himself faced with another proposal from Martin Harcourt as they sat in the pub the next afternoon.

"Sometimes we get asked to do some work that's a bit beyond our scope," he said to Perry over a pint in the Boatswain. "We've got forensic accountants we work with, of course, but this one is a bit more - " he searched for an expression " - needing someone in on the ground. Taking a look around."

Perry had no idea what a forensic accountant was. He got that a lot with Martin, who never seemed to realise his legal jargon was a different language. He said nothing and waited for Martin to continue.

"The client's a partner at the Brewery. It seems Arthur Stanton didn't own it outright, he'd taken on a partner a few years back. Now he's dead and they're going through the books, it looks like there's been some funny business. The partner wants to know where the money is."

It sounded way beyond Perry's league. "He can't go to the police?"

"Right now it's more of an internal matter. We can't say for certain that there has been fraud, but it looks that way."

"You need me to break in and get you some papers, that sort of thing?" Perry asked.

"No, we've got all those. What we really need is someone to go in and have a sniff around. See if anyone's moving stock where they shouldn't. Not the odd crate, but larger amounts. You could go in at the warehouse, as a casual, then just keep an eye out."

Perry toyed with a beer mat, tipping it on its edge and rotating it so that each side tapped against the table in turn. He was wondering whether it was the sort of work he wanted to get into. It sounded a bit close to informing.

"You think about it anyway. The money's not bad." He named a figure, looking for a reaction, but Perry's face didn't move a muscle.

Eventually he said: "I'll think on it."

It was a figure so large he couldn't just dismiss it. With that and the money for the photographs job, he'd have nearly enough for the new engine. He'd have to mull it over.

Frankie Goodlock was still having woes with her plant shipment and had gone down to Bristol to try and sort it out.

In her absence Barney had started grafting fruit trees. He already had a load of bud sticks wrapped in moist burlap, and he was carefully loosening the bark of the rootstock and slipping them in. If tropical plants were Frankie's passion, Barney's was fruit trees. He was trying to start a line in multiple grafts: peaches, plums and apricots all on the same stem. It was a long term project as many of his experiments needed years to establish.

"These ones are all Torinel," he told Perry, referring to the name of the rootstock. "We'll move them down to the far end. They'll all need staking."

It had been hot with no rain for days so there was plenty of watering needed for the thirsty display plants. Barney was also trying to fix the irrigation system for the beds. He and Frankie had installed a drip irrigation system as it was more water efficient and they were trying to run the nursery along sustainable lines. It had turned into a headache: the tubes and valves frequently getting blocked, and springing leaks that were hard to detect.

"Want me to take a look at the irrigation?" Perry offered.

"If you like. I'll finish up these," Barney said.

Perry made some checks. "You've had rats or mice, I reckon."

"I suspected as much. We'll have to try and get rid of them. You know Frankie though, can't stand for killing animals."

"You could try peppermint. Don't know if it works for rats, though." Peppermint oil had been Black Bessie's weapon of choice against the infestations of mice they encountered in some of the seedier digs they stayed in.

Barney stood up from the grafting, putting down his pruning knife. "Anything's worth a go. I've half a mind to give up on the whole system. The rainfall's usually enough anyway."

"I don't know why you put it in to begin with. Must have been a pricey business," Perry said.

Barney agreed. "It was. But Frankie wanted to find a way to use the old well. We had the water tested and it was only fit for the garden."

The two men set to replacing the damaged irrigation tubing.

"I might need to swap a couple of shifts around next week," Perry said. He had finally come to a decision about Martin's offer and decided he couldn't afford to pass it up. "Martin put some work my way. Just for a week or so."

Barney finished splicing in a new section. "That'll be no problem. He's alright, Martin. Solid."

Perry thought so too, or he'd never have taken the work on. He still feared he was getting in out of his depth. What did he know about spying on some business?

"See you down the Boatswain later?" he asked Barney as he left.

"Not tonight. Too much to do with Frankie gone. Pass on my regards to the usual crowd."

It was Ray and Priscilla behind the bar that night. "Mary's got to look after the kid," he told Perry. "It's turned out to be quite a situation. Social workers threatening all sorts if she's left by herself. Mary's too damn soft-hearted, getting us into this. Now we're stuck with the brat. Though she's a good kid, I'll grant you," he added. "No trouble really."

Perry remembered himself at twelve. He and Jake, roaming around and getting up to all sorts. Involved in Company business. It was different for girls, he supposed. Social took more care with them. After all there were worse things that could happen to a young girl. God forbid she ever started running around with the wrong crowd and ending up in a detention centre like he had.

Priscilla wasn't in the best of moods. Ray was a harder taskmaster than Mary and chivvied the staff along if they spent too much time flirting with customers, which to Priscilla was one of the few perks of the job. She'd ditched the boyfriend she was seeing a while ago and had an eye out for a replacement. She liked Perry well enough but she was out for a guy with a car and prospects.

All in all the atmosphere was flat. Perry decided to call it a night. He was limiting himself to one drink most nights, saving up for the narrowboat engine. He also didn't want to end up like the fat old geezers who spent all their days propping up the bar.

Walking back home he got to thinking about a campfire, remembering Rose's words. It wasn't a bad idea. He might catch a couple of perch. Flies with a streak of orange, they liked, and bug eyes. He had some of those left in a packet: tiny brass barbells that you made eyes with. Perry had gleaned most of his fly fishing knowledge from anglers up and down the riverbank. Back in the day he'd gone fishing because it was a cheap meal in leaner times.

Just as he left the Boatswain he glimpsed the dark figure of a woman hurrying through the garden at the back. For a moment he could have sworn it was Mary, but what would she be doing out at this hour?

Juvenile detention had been the darkest period in Perry's life. He had one goal: to keep his head down, survive it, and get out.

It was brutal. The staff were sadists. Perry was one of the most exemplary detainees they'd ever had but it was still never good enough. Bullying and violence were rife among the boys detained there as well. Perry, then skinnier and smaller than others in his age group, was an obvious target.

But he was stronger than he looked, and nimble. He easily survived a clumsy assault by one of the "chiefs" - a hulking lad who was inside for his second stint - leaving the larger boy with a black eye and a split lip. Perry was pretty much left alone after this.

He had no visitors. No family came to see him during visiting hours. Though he wasn't alone in this, most of the other boys coming from backgrounds of broken homes and neglect. Others had family who couldn't afford the time or travel costs to visit them.

The brutality was masked by a veneer of rehabilitation: social workers and education and preparing to get boys into trades when they were released. But the reality was that no one cared about them. They were written off.

There was one social worker who stood out from the others, Trudy, a black woman. She seemed to be interested in Perry for a while. She found out that he read books when he could, and got him some. She was encouraging him to get back into education. Get himself some O-levels or CSEs.

Trudy had a nephew who was doing electrical engineering and she thought something like that might suit Perry as he liked doing things with his hands and he was a smart boy.

But then she got transferred and the one who replaced her didn't follow any of it up. None of them could really be bothered. They expected most of the kids would be back inside again anyway within a few months of release.

12

"The orders come in here, see, and then you load up the designated lorry. It all gets checked off before the driver leaves, and then you mark it off in this book."

From his first morning working in the Brewery warehouse, Perry couldn't see anything obviously wrong. Of course a little bit of stock went by-the-by here and there, but that was to be expected. Even Ray and Mary never managed to reconcile everything perfectly when they did a stocktake. It was the way of things.

Brewery staff could also buy beer at cost price, and Arthur Stanton hadn't been stingy about handing out a free crate here and there, such as for an anniversary. Perry found this out from the start as the day he arrived was some bloke's birthday.

"You'll be taking your free crate home then, Fred?"

"Happen I will."

"We'll drop by round yours later, give you a hand drinking it."

All of this largesse helped keep theft down. It wasn't worth anyone's while to be ripping the business off as working conditions and pay weren't bad. If you got sacked for stealing, your chances of finding another situation would be tough. Perry remembered the shifty looking Grover bloke. That might be a line of inquiry to follow up, he thought.

One obstacle he faced when digging for information was a general wariness among the staff. A boss dropping dead and the subsequent uncertainty over the future of the company and their jobs was bad enough. Add to this the frequent visits and interviews by the police, and nerves had been put on edge. They weren't ready to take a newcomer into their confidence.

Perry knew these things took time. He was happy to be patient, so long as the client could wait.

After a couple of days he had the processes and systems figured out. He could see where there were weak links but he couldn't see where any of them were being exploited. Financial fraud would take place higher up the line and Harcourts had people looking at that. So while he could have broken into the offices after hours and sifted through desks and drawers, there was no need.

Whatever it was, he didn't think it was in the warehouse. In the bottling plant, maybe. He'd have to try to get them to move him there.

Perry had found out that several of the Brewery workers played darts together, so at the end of the week he joined them at their local haunt. It was a dingy place on the eastern outskirts of the city.

He had some skill with darts, a legacy of his fairground days when he and the other lads would practice on the stall games after hours. The ones who ran the games had to be good so they could make it look easy and lure the punters in. Perry could also hold his own with a miniature crossbow or an airgun with dodgy sights.

Showing some prowess at darts won him the approval of the other Brewery men, and from there a bit more trust. A couple of rounds of beers also saw tongues loosened. Perry won further acceptance by getting in the second round.

"You're living down on the canal, so I heard?" one bloke asked him. He had a tattoo of a rose and a skull on his upper arm.

Perry acknowledged this.

"Brother-in-law of mine had a boat, for holidays. Nasty business with the toilet, always clogging. His missus threatened to walk if he didn't sell it," the tattooed man said.

"I'd have sold the missus and sailed off on the boat!" another one interrupted, slapping his pint mug on the table. There was a raucous chorus of approval.

"Must be nice to be free, upping sticks as soon as you've a mind to." This speaker was Fred, who had a thin and lugubrious face. He looked wistful as he spoke.

"Not if he's got the handcuffs on. You got yourself a ball and chain yet, Perry?" the joker asked. From the size of his beer gut he looked like a heavy ball himself. He was strong though. Perry had seen him lifting the heaviest loads of all the men.

Perry confessed that he hadn't got a woman.

"You keep it that way, lad. Nothing but trouble once that all starts." There were several nods in agreement as the rose-and-skull man spoke.

"You won't get a woman living on a boat. Not the sort of woman that you'd want to having living on your boat, at any rate!" The beer-bellied joker won another roar of laughter.

"How long you planning on stopping, then?" Thin-faced Fred was interested in the idea of a house boat. "Got plans for where you'll move to next?"

Perry used this to get the subject back to the Brewery. "Might stop for a while. Seems like a good situation here, while there's work."

The joker sobered up. "Could be worse. If we're not all out by Christmas."

"Not likely, is it?" Perry asked.

"Who knows? There's always talk of layoffs. Doesn't help with the boss popping his clogs. Or someone popping them for him, rather." He raised his fingers to his head, imitating the sound of a trigger click.

"And his missus too. Funny thing that were," Fred said.

"They never replaced Grover with a permanent, did they?" the tattooed man pointed out. "Just casuals like you, Perry. Don't have to pay the benefits then, do they? No holiday or sick pay."

"Ah but Grover was different. Big row there was. Old Stanton might have tried to hush it up but there was something odd going on."

"You're always seeing conspiracies, Fred. Grover was as bent as a fork." The joker stood up. "My round, boys. Same again?" He trundled off to the bar leaving Fred looking piqued.

"It was odd," he muttered, more to himself than anyone. "Him showing up that night."

"What's that, Fred?" the tattooed man asked.

But Fred was now discouraged. "Nothing much. Ask no questions, tell no lies." He drained the rest of his drink, waiting for the new one to arrive.

Perry had guessed right about Grover. There was something there. Getting it out of Fred might be a lengthy process though, if he even knew anything worthwhile.

It was around a five mile walk back home, taking Perry through the centre of the city on the most direct route. A month or so ago the roads would have been thronging with students at this hour: spilling out of the bars, staggering back drunk over Magdalen Bridge, singing and making a racket. Tonight it was comparatively peaceful.

As he finally reached the canal a weight he hadn't known he was carrying fell off him. He'd reached sanctuary. He hadn't realised how much on edge he'd been, with the new workmates in the unfamiliar pub. Probably because they weren't really his workmates, it was just a front for him. Maybe he wasn't cut out for this kind of work, spying and snooping around.

There was a short cut he could take through some allotments. They locked the gates at night but that didn't prevent Perry from getting through. Picking the gate lock, a simple business, soothed his nerves. He felt in control of his situation again. He was in his own dimension.

The allotments were unlit and shadowy but the moon was bright enough and it shaved a few minutes off the journey. He couldn't see what vegetables were growing but he could smell the dry, dusty fragrance of tomato plants. They always smelt like a warm day in the sun. Barney often put a few vegetables Perry's way from his own patch. He and Frankie grew more than they needed.

Finally Perry was home on his own soil, or rather the wooden deck of the Emerald, and he felt a deep gladness. He put all thoughts of the day out of his mind.

Instead with the aid of his battery lamp he looked at some maps of the waterways. He should move on, he told himself, once this job was done. Barney and Frankie wouldn't find it hard to replace him at the nursery.

He'd miss it, though. He hadn't intended to start putting down roots but he realised he had been getting settled. Meeting up with the same crowd in the Boatswain most evenings, getting to know other people's business, becoming known himself.

The brewery blokes were right: having no ties was easiest. If he did start dating someone he'd get stuck there. He could hardly see Priscilla going up the river with him. Come to think of it he couldn't really see her on the boat at all. He wasn't at all sure if he wasn't going off the idea altogether. Maybe he simply valued his freedom too much.

Perry got released early for good behaviour. Freedom, finally. By then he was sixteen and although he was still a minor, no one really cared much what he did. He soon found that the world viewed him as a "borstal boy" and the cards were all stacked against him whatever he tried.

So he left town and set off by himself.

He was free. He had nothing and no one, and no door - quite literally, thanks to his gift with locks - was closed to him.

Yet the lure of easy money wasn't enough for Perry once he got out. It wasn't even that he'd seen the consequences, or feared a similar fate to Jake. It was that he was sick of being beholden to them all.

And truth be told, other than he loved the adrenalin and the satisfaction of a lock yielding to him, of that click-and-twist moment when he finally tried the handle and a door was opened to him, he'd never had much of a taste for the business.

This was the start of his roaming days. He turned his back on the towns and the cities and made for the countryside.

13

Perry had his sights set on Grover. The ex-Brewery employee was his next line of inquiry. If anyone had been meddling or fiddling about, it stood to reason that he was the culprit. Otherwise why fire him?

He wasn't the only one to reach this conclusion. The police also thought they had their suspect for the murders. George Grover, disgruntled former employee of the Brewery, had been heard arguing with Arthur Stanton after his dismissal and "sounding like he was making threats".

When detectives visited Grover's digs they found bullets of the type used to kill Arthur and Sybil. It all seemed pretty conclusive: motive, means, evidence. No apparent alibi.

The only problem was that Grover had disappeared. Gone to ground.

There were notices put out in the paper with a photo fit of him. They warned the public to stay away if they did spot him, since he was armed, and offered a reward for any information leading to his arrest.

"Doesn't look much like him, does it?" Perry said when they were handing the newspaper around in the pub.

"You knew him?" Barney asked.

"Saw him once over at your place. Looking for work."

Barney turned to Frankie for corroboration. She nodded. "I sent him away. We had nothing available, anyway."

"Was this before or after the widow was killed?" Barney asked.

Perry had to think about it. "Before, I think. Quite a bit before."

Despite what the police thought, and the rumours at the Brewery, Perry didn't think Grover had done it. Why would he be hanging around if he'd just got away with doing someone in? He'd have been off, unless he was half-witted.

Or unless he needed to kill the widow first.

It didn't fit. Him turning up at the nursery to ask for work wasn't in keeping with a killer planning a second hit.

The arrest warrant created another dilemma for Perry. Now the police were after Grover, Perry's pursuit of him aligned his goals with the police's goals. This was not a situation he was comfortable with. It felt perilously close to working with them, even though he had a different paymaster. He could only imagine what King John's lot would say.

A second dilemma was Priscilla. As soon as Perry had decided not to bother pursuing that course, she switched all her attention to him. Whether it coincided with her finally giving up on Martin he couldn't say. But Perry was busy now and didn't need any distractions.

"There's a band playing at the Stag on Thursday. Why don't we make a night of it?"

This was addressed solely to Perry, as he was the only one at the bar. If he said "maybe some other time", which was what he wanted to say, then that would be that. She'd take it as a snub no matter how kindly he tried to put it.

She was a good girl after all, and nice looking. It seemed like a waste to pass it up.

"Why not?"

Priscilla didn't jump for joy at his acceptance but she looked satisfied enough. "I'll meet you there at eight then. They're playing from nine."

It was more or less a date.

"I hear you're doing some work with Martin Harcourt," Priscilla said.

Was this the reason for her sudden interest? Perry wondered.

"A few odd jobs. Who said so?"

"Martin did. Said you were doing private inquiry work for his uncle's firm," Priscilla told him. She sounded impressed by it.

Perry had a suspicious feeling that Martin had been trying to put a good word in for him. Still, he wasn't one to look a gift horse in the mouth. "Something like that," he said.

"Is that why you've started those shifts at the Brewery? Are you trying to track down the killer?"

Her eyes were gleaming with interest now and Perry felt a bit sickened, though he couldn't put his finger on why.

"That's for the police to sort out. It's something else I'm doing." Priscilla clearly wanted to know more but he wasn't going to tell her. He expected her to tell him that the date was off, but she didn't. Instead she gave him a knowing smile and went down the far end of the bar to serve another customer.

Perry realised she didn't believe him. She thought he was bluffing, and that in actual fact he was working as some sort of private detective. Then when he thought about it some more, he realised he kind of was.

Rose had attached herself firmly to Dilys. Although Mary was officially looking after her, Rose spent most days accompanying Dilys to her various cleaning jobs. Dilys didn't mind, and even had Rose help her out with small tasks.

"You ought to be careful, Dill. You don't want to get done for child labour. And nor do I." Mary was only half joking.

"It keeps her occupied. Besides, they're useful skills you're learning, aren't they, Rose?"

Rose grinned. "I can do hospital corners."

"Old Mrs Crawshaw won't stand for fitted sheets and she's a stickler for order," Dilys explained.

"You'd better not show her your room then. If Dilys is teaching you all these things, maybe you should keep your things in better order? I don't think you've made your bed since you've been here."

Rose merely laughed at Mary. She was a much happier child than she had been a couple of weeks ago. She was surrounded by people who didn't resent her and were kinder to her than her late father and stepmother had been.

It had been arranged that she'd stay on there for the summer, then go north to her relatives and start at a new school in September. The woman of the house, a cousin of Rose's late mother, had been down to visit. She had daughters some years older than Rose and seemed alright, from what Mary said, and Rose didn't seem to have taken against her. The cousin was able to take Rose straight away if need be, but she worked as a nurse and would have to arrange holiday care. So it made better sense for Rose to move up when school began.

This suited Rose, who wanted to remain where she was. Mary anticipated having a battle on her hands at the end of August but had agreed to let Rose stay.

Once or twice Rose had come down to the canal to visit Perry. He didn't mind her hanging around but he avoided letting her inside the boat.

"Can you swim, Rosie?" he asked, anxious when she sat dangling her feet over the edge of the canal.

"Of course I can!" She was scornful.

"Even so, don't go so close to the edge. There's thick weeds and that in the water. You might get trapped. Broken glass and other junk too."

Rose deliberately leaned her foot down even further, trying to reach the water. "You'd save me though, wouldn't you, Perry Beck?"

"I'd have a go saving anyone who fell in," he told her.

"But if it was me and all the others fallen in, you'd save me first, wouldn't you?"

He laughed. "Only because you're a kid, and the others would be stronger swimmers."

"I'm strong. I lift stuff all the time with Dilys. She says I'm a good worker. She reckons I could easily get a job if I was old enough."

"You should finish school first," Perry said. It gave you a lot more options. He didn't exactly regret dropping out himself, because he'd always managed to find work, but an education gave you more opportunities.

It was late summer when Perry had headed for the countryside and there was plenty of farm labour about as the harvesting started. Cash in hand, no questions asked, so long as you could put in the hard hours you'd be hired.

Perry dossed down with other seasonal workers in temporary camps, eventually buying his own tent off a bloke who was moving on. He grew brown and strong with the labour. He liked the open air work. He still had a horror of being shut up.

The winter was tougher and it grew freezing to camp. He'd be bundled up with two old sleeping bags and whatever blankets he'd managed to get his hands on, and he'd still wake like ice in the morning. In the end he and another lad, Michael, got work cutting Christmas trees. It was a better situation as there was a shed for them to sleep in.

He was drawn to Oxfordshire. It felt like home even though he had no intentions of tracking down the Company.

He had to be a bit careful because he was still a minor and there were some that might give him more of a hassle about this. He could have easily picked a few locks to get money and food but he reasoned it was better to stay on the right side of the law.

From what they'd warned him about probation and early release, it would take one step out of line for him to get sent straight back there.

14

It was a turnabout of events. Perry needed information and for that he needed the Company.

He kicked himself for not having got the details of their current address when they had visited him. Though of course he hadn't needed them then. Tracking them down when he did want them was not so easy, but there were the usual places they haunted. He only needed to drop word and it would reach them.

Taking a bus to Faringdon, a market town half way between Oxford and Swindon, he made his way to the Hampden Pye. The headless figure of the pub's ghostly namesake swung from the inn's sign. "Come and Meet Faringdon's Famous Ghost!" a poster proclaimed, advertising tours of the supposedly haunted graveyard.

Inside the public bar the beady old woman pulling ale gave Perry a sharp glance. "It's been some years since you were here, son."

He'd been a boy the last time. It was nearly a decade ago that the Company had taken temporary residence in the town and frequented the Hampden. He was disconcerted the old woman remembered him.

"I don't forget a face, when they're one of John's boys," she said. "Not with those eyes of yours, anyhow."

Perry ordered a half. "Been seeing much action?" he asked.

"Quiet as the grave these past months. You still working with them?" The landlady pushed the handle back up and put the glass in front of him.

"Got my own gig in Oxford now. Different line of work."

"Ooo, fancy. A professor at one of them colleges, are you?"

Perry grinned. "I've not gone gown yet."

"So what are you doing in these parts?" She asked but she had already guessed, Perry thought.

"Just stopping by. Always nice to catch up with old friends, if they drop in."

The old woman understood. If any of the Company came in, she'd send them Perry's way.

He took his drink to a quiet corner, keeping an eye out. Some crony would show up eventually. He was doing a lot of waiting around and biding his time, so it seemed to him. Paid work it might be, but it was taking up his time.

There was a lot to get sorted on the Emerald. He was due to pump out the waste and refill the water tank, which he did at a nearby boatyard. It would be an unpleasant business if he were late with that.

Sure enough a rat-faced little fellow came into the Hampden within the hour. He had two other men with him. They sat at the other end of the room, but when the rat-faced man went to the bar to order drinks, Perry saw the landlady indicating his way.

The little man approached Perry's table. "It's a fine afternoon, isn't it? You drinking alone?"

"Could always welcome company," Perry said, emphasising the last word.

"Ah, company." With the meaning quite clear, the other man pulled up a stool. "And how might I be of service, as a fellow Kingsman, so I do believe?"

Perry had no time for cryptic conversation. "I need to get hold of King John. He mentioned he was down Swindon way when he last dropped by."

"So he is. You'd be in luck then, since the moon is full."

Perry remembered King John's odd quirk of holding Company meetings at a full moon. King John claimed it was because a bright moon made a poor night for thieving. Or adventure, as he preferred to call it. Perry suspected it was more about pageantry than convenience. The first Sunday or second Tuesday of a given month would have done just as well.

If the Company were congregating that night, so much the better. Even if King John didn't come good with any information on Grover one of the others might have something.

Perry had been given the name of a dingy pub in a suburban street in Swindon. He didn't know Swindon, he couldn't remember having ever gone there. By evening he managed to locate the place and get himself admitted to the backroom where King John Lochinvar was holding his monthly court.

Perry remembered these meetings from the old days. They were an excuse to meet, drink and gamble more than anything. At least that was how most of the Company viewed them. For King John they were an invaluable source of information, with members bringing in the latest news from different areas. He would use this information to decide his future strategy: what operations should be carried out where, and by whom.

Proceedings tonight weren't very active. A couple of lads were playing dice in the corner. Perry nodded to them. In the centre of the room King John sat at the head of a long table. Old Owen hovered behind his chair, not doing very much at all. The boy Joe was nowhere to be seen.

His eyes brightened when he saw Perry. "Beck lad! Seen some sense at last?"

"Not that, John." He came straight to the point. "It's information I'm after."

"Ah, well. Information comes at a price, doesn't it?" King John was about to start bargaining but something about Perry's steady gaze unnerved him. "But for you, being as you're family, I'm sure we can come to some arrangement."

"Fellow named Grover." Perry gave a brief description.

King John's eyes narrowed. "And why would you be interested in a cove like that? Wanted for murder, isn't he?"

So King John did know of him. "Reasons," Perry said.

The eyes bored into him. "Not gone over, have you, Beck? Turned snitch?"

"As if. It's a private client. Co-owner of the Brewery where that bloke was shot." Perry saw no harm in revealing this. King John might sniff out something useful. "Money's missing. Doesn't want the publicity of the coppers coming in."

King John was silent for a while, considering.

"He's not one of our lot, but you'd know that. He's from Basingstoke way."

"What's his game?" Perry asked.

"A bit of this, a bit of that. Uncle had some dealings with him back in the days of the Cowley gang."

King John indicated Old Owen, who stepped closer. "He was a forger. And a bad one." Old Owen's voice came out in a wheeze.

"Gave you some trouble, didn't he Uncle, over those queer screens?" King John referred to counterfeit bank notes.

"That he did. Couldn't pass them anywhere." Old Owen looked sorrowful over this long ago memory.

Perry was wondering where these talents might have been employed at the Brewery, and what connection - if any - there was to Arthur Stanton. That side of things might not be his concern but he found himself increasingly thinking about it.

"He's not in that line of work anymore, at any rate. It's years since I've come across him anywhere," King John said. "Then all of a sudden he's in the papers and you come in asking about him, Beck. You can see how it looks."

Perry felt wearied of it all. "Like I said, it's a private job. Nothing to do with Thames Valley." He meant the Thames Valley police who were responsible for policing Oxfordshire and a couple of neighbouring counties. He changed the subject. "Is Bessie around?"

"Been a good long while since you saw her, Beck lad, hasn't it?"

Perry supposed this was so. "Is she here?"

"Not tonight. You remember her Tina?" Perry did. The mixed race daughter who shunned the Company, preferring instead to live with a father and stepmother in Milton Keynes, and then working in a respectable office.

"She's just had a kiddie. Bessie's gone to stay with her. I'll be sure to pass on your regards, though."

Just then a couple of other Company members arrived. King John greeted them warmly. "Ah, the boys from Banbury. Things any better on your patch?"

"Not so much action there, John. Getting nasty in Coventry and Milton," one of them told him. "Turf wars among some of the dealers."

"That's far beyond our concern," King John said.

"Maybe, but there's word it's coming from this way. Pushing prices down."

"We've got no distribution beyond Oxford, boys. It's not from us it's coming."

Perry was sickened that the Company had got into the drugs trade. He'd seen what it had done to a few of the kids he'd known. Mind you if they couldn't get harder stuff they'd sniff aerosols and glue. It all did for them in the end. Still, it wasn't a business that King John would have gone for in the old days.

Perry had got what he came for, so he made his exit.

Tina had been a quiet girl. A few years older than him, not so old as Jake though. She'd been nice to him when he was little though she wasn't with them very often. Her father wasn't having any of that. He was a taxi driver and anything between him and Black Bessie had been over years ago. He and his new wife were respectable people who didn't want Tina associating with her mother's kin.

Tina had been a schoolgirl when Perry had first been with the Company. He knew this, because his only real memory was of her sitting on the floor cross legged, noticing her knees were a different colour to his knees above her long grey school socks.

By the time he returned to the Company after the years in foster care she had left school and was working. Black Bessie took Jake and him to visit her one day. It was in an office in some sort of business. Perry's most vivid recollection was of how exasperated Tina was by her mother's presence, how she clearly wanted the three of them to leave. He couldn't remember, if he had ever known, what Black Bessie's motive was in going.

What he did remember afterwards was how smart and clean it all was, and how smart Tina's clothes were. And how he could see that there was the Company's world and the other world, and that Tina was part of the other world.

15

Perry had put on a clean shirt for his date with Priscilla at the White Stag. Laundry was a tricky business on a boat, particularly with no electricity and thus no washing machine. If he ever got the Emerald wired up he had an idea to put in a twin tub, but it wasn't high on his list of priorities.

If he couldn't be bothered to go to a laundrette, or the weather was too wet for drying after a hand wash, Dilys would sometimes do a bag of clothes for him.

He'd asked her especially to iron him a shirt in the last batch. "What's the special occasion, then?"

"Just going out." She'd find out soon enough but he didn't want a load of hassle beforehand.

Perry got to the White Stag a few minutes early and Priscilla arrived ten minutes late. She was wearing a shorter skirt than she usually wore in the Boatswain, and a blouse with a much lower neckline. She wasn't as full as Mary up top but she had enough to be going on with, Perry thought. He saw other blokes looking at her with admiring eyes and felt fortunate to be the one meeting her.

"Hello Perry," she greeted him. "Nice evening for it, isn't it?"

He had managed to get a table outside. The place was already filling up, the local band playing had a following and there would be a large crowd of townsfolk and pleasure boaters there that night.

Priscilla held the table while Perry got the first drinks in. He had a beer, she had a Bacardi and coke. He sat down with her, at a bit of a loss.

"So tell me about yourself, Perry," she asked.

He was stumped by that one because he figured she knew everything there was to know about him. Everything she needed to know, anyway. What he did, where he lived. Who he hung out with.

She helped him out. "You grew up local, then?"

He had. All around the place. "My mum died when I was a baby, so there was some foster care and moving about. All around the area, though." Except for the spell inside and he wasn't going to bring that up.

"Yes, I heard about your mum. Sad, that."

Where had she heard it from? Perry couldn't remember mentioning it. He had told Dilys once, when she'd asked him if he went back to his family for Christmas. It struck him that Dilys probably related everything he said back to Priscilla and Mary and everyone else.

"It was before I could remember it. How about you?"

Before Priscilla could answer two of the bar staff came by the outdoor tables, wielding an enormous tray of sausages, burgers and chicken drumsticks. "Meat tray raffle! Just a quid a ticket. Perfume and branded sunglasses for second and third prize."

"You ought to go in for that, Perry," Priscilla said. "The perfume might be nice even if you didn't win the meat."

Perry had no need for a tray of nearly expired meat. The perfume and sunshades, along with the meat, had almost certainly fallen off the back of a lorry. But he didn't want to look stingy and he could see that Priscilla wanted a chance at the scent. He tried to buy a single ticket but the man jostled him to put a whole fiver in. "Best quality meat this, from Stan's Premium Meats. Worth well over a hundred quid."

If it had been prime steak and peacock breast it wouldn't have been worth a hundred quid, given the state it was in. Perry handed over the money and the man tore him off five flimsy raffle tickets. Priscilla took them. "We'll have to remember these numbers, for when they call."

As the meat tray men moved onto another table, Perry spied Dilys sitting over with some people on another table, Mary's brother Damon among them. Perry lowered his head, hoping Dilys wouldn't spot them. Of course she did, and came over.

"Hello Perry, didn't expect to see you here. You here for the band?" She looked from him to Priscilla. "Date night, is it? About time."

Priscilla smirked and Perry shifted in his seat.

"You here with Damon, then?" Priscilla asked.

"Not likely. Just happened to all end up at the same table," Dilys said. Wearing a sundress she looked ten years younger than she did in her cleaning gear. She was attractive, Perry thought, if not his type. Fair, like Mary, but with more of a tawny shade to her hair.

He had hoped the band would be playing indoors so the sound wouldn't drown them, but worse luck, they were playing outside. Far too loudly. The White Stag was always getting noise complaints. It meant he couldn't easily sustain a conversation with Priscilla. Then he considered that perhaps this was for the best, since he didn't really know what to say to her. Outside the setting of the Boatswain it all seemed to dry up. People talked about films, he supposed, and television shows, but he didn't get into much of that living on the boat. He was cut off.

So they sat and watched the band, drinking and sharing a basket of chips. Perry bought most of it. It wasn't his kind of music.

When the musicians took a break, the barman came onto the microphone to announce the raffle. Priscilla was grasping the tickets, hoping for one of their numbers to be called.

"For the luxury brand sunglasses, third prize, red ticket seventy-four."

Perry's and Priscilla's tickets were green.

"This designer perfume, straight from gay Paree, green ticket nineteen."

Priscilla looked disappointed. They had numbers sixty to sixty-four.

"And our top prize of the evening, our tray of premium meats, courtesy of Stan's Premium Meats down in the Covered Market - don't forget to stop by there for your Sunday joint - green ticket sixty-three."

Perry's heart sank but Priscilla looked pleased. "You've won, Perry! Your luck must be in tonight."

"I bought the tickets for both of us. Why don't you take it?"

But Priscilla had even less interest in the meat than Perry did. "I couldn't possibly, you bought the tickets. Besides, what use would I have for all that meat? You'd need a whole family to get through that lot."

The same went for Perry, but he said nothing. He thought the best thing to do was just to leave it there.

Unfortunately when they were leaving, the barman spotted him and foisted the tray of meat on him. "Nearly forgot your prize, sir! You'll enjoy a week's worth of meals with all that."

Perry was forced to carry the tray all the way back. He had planned to put his arm around Priscilla but now he was stuck with the meat. Priscilla didn't seem to care. She chattered about a few things as he walked her back to her place. Just as he was figuring out whether he should put the tray down and kiss her goodnight, and if so, where he should set it, she turned from unlocking her door and said: "That was a nice night, Perry. We should do it again sometime. I'll see you down the Boatswain."

"Night then." Not knowing what else to say, he turned with his tray of meat and walked homewards.

It was a warm night and Perry had nowhere cold to store the meat. He half thought about chucking it in the canal. Instead he left it on the deck, hoping someone might nick it and take the problem out of his hands.

But when he rose, early, there it was waiting for him. Big and sweaty and meaty, a greenish sheen on several of the items. It looked even nastier than it had done the previous night. He decided to offload it on Ray and Mary, and hauled it to the Boatswain.

"We might have a barbecue with it," Mary said.

"It's been out all night," Perry cautioned.

Mary went to take a proper look at the meat. "I don't know when it died, Perry, but I'd be dating it somewhere last century. It's about an hour away from going high. You'd better get rid of it or the police will think there's a corpse in here. And God knows we've had enough of those this past month."

"Can I chuck it in the bins round the back?"

"Why not. They're emptied tomorrow. Wrap it in a couple of bin liners first, so it doesn't stink the place out."

Perry did so. It wasn't as bad as fish at least, you really couldn't leave them out too long. He'd quickly learnt this lesson the first time he'd had some fish and not been able to store them properly.

Coming back into the bar, deciding he needed an early drink to cleanse himself of the meat, Perry saw Damon in the corner. He looked like he'd been out all night and slept in his clothes. Which he probably had.

He waved Perry over and Perry pulled up a chair. Damon stank of weed as usual. It was always a bit of a mystery what he did for a living. Supposedly something in theatre, but he seemed to spend all his time mooching off Mary.

"I heard you've got some work down the Brewery," he said to Perry. "What's it like down there?"

"Not so bad. Pay's reasonable," Perry told him.

"Reckon they've got any more casual shifts going?"

Perry was surprised by the question. He looked at Damon, his thin fingers rolling a Rizla around a pinch of tobacco, and wondered what on earth a bloke like that would want with hauling crates. He was hardly the type for manual work.

"I could ask," he offered.

"Thanks." Damon didn't give any reason as to why he needed the work and Perry didn't ask.

Perry kept on the straight as far as he could. He looked for legitimate ways to get by. One day he found an old rod in a junk shop and managed to fix it up for a few quid. He had no idea how to fish so he hung out by the river, watching other people fishing and trying to copy what they did.

A couple of old anglers took pity on him - after having a good laugh at his efforts - and gave him some bait. They showed him the ropes and he also found out from them about tying flies.

"Fiddly, they are," one of the old fellows said, but Perry thought he might give it a go. Hooks and cotton were cheap, and he could get feathers for free from a local butcher. Pheasant plumes were the best, he discovered. In the early days he scavenged for materials, picking up stray bits of tinsel from Christmas decorations to add some flash.

He had deft hands and a good eye for it. He found he enjoyed making the flies, more than the fishing. He'd sometimes barter them for a bit of fish. Later he found out that anglers would actually pay money for them. A tiny amount, but it bought a can of drink or a packet of crisps.

Most of all he loved the water. It was like a road, with all the river traffic flowing up and down it, but much slower and more peaceful.

16

Perry got talking to Fred from the Brewery during a tea break. He'd detected some interest in boats in the other man, and thought this might open up a conversation.

"You done much boating?" he asked as they sat on a couple of crates round the back of the warehouse.

Fred was unwrapping cling film from a squashed cheese sandwich. "Not since I were a lad. Had an auntie on the Isle of Wight, where we used to go sailing. A long time ago now."

"Not thought of taking it up again?"

"Often. The wife won't have it though, thinks we ought to go on one of them cruises. But being holed up with a load of people, ferried around on a set course, it's not the same, is it?"

Perry agreed that it wasn't. "You can set your own pace on the waterways."

"That you can. I've been wondering about them narrowboats. Just for a holiday. Can't see as I'd get the missus aboard, though."

"You're welcome to come down and take a look at my boat," Perry said. "She's not moving much at the moment, needs a new motor."

Fred's eyes brightened. "That'd be something. Whereabouts you moored?"

Perry told him. It was arranged for Fred to stop by the following day, which was Saturday. Perry figured once Fred was down there, he could get him to the Boatswain and pour a few beers into him. Away from the other brewery blokes, he might lose his inhibitions and loosen his tongue.

He'd also asked a manager about shifts for Damon.

"Have you worked with him before?" the manager asked. "Is he any use?" He'd been stung before by blokes' useless mates.

Perry couldn't answer this honestly and he didn't want to look a fool through lying. The minute Damon turned up they'd see him for what he was. "He wants the work," he said.

The manager had been pleased enough with Perry's efforts so far, and decided to take a punt on his friend. "I'll see what we can do. Have him come down Tuesday. We've got the big deliveries going out then."

That was Damon sorted, Perry thought. Given he'd be leaving himself soon, if he managed to get anything out of Fred, there'd be an opening anyway. He could only imagine what the others would make of Damon and his velvet coats.

Perry had managed to get a good look over the bottling plant since he had been working there. It was an interesting process watching the bottles go along the line through the filler and finally get capped, labelled and packed.

Stanton's Traditional, Stanton's Pale Ale, Stanton's Old Peculiar, Stanton's Premium Gold. Then the quirkier lines for the younger crowd and the tourists: Stanton's Old Tom, Stanton's Dreaming Spires. These last two had paintings of Oxford's skyline on their labels, and weren't sold much beyond the city and its surrounds.

No one minded Perry having a look.

"Impressive, isn't it? The first time you see it," one of the plant workers remarked.

It was. The speed, regularity and rhythm of everything going along were hypnotic. All the gleaming bottles travelling past. But Perry couldn't linger long. He needed to get back to the loading area and pull his weight there.

Frankie's bromeliads had finally arrived when Perry arrived to do a couple of hours work later that day. He'd had to juggle things around due to working in the Brewery in the mornings. For all the anticipation, the specimens that Frankie was unloading weren't all that impressive in Perry's view. They just looked like leaves. Long, dark green and shiny. There were any amount of English plants that looked that good or better.

"They're supposed to be all these bright colours, once they bloom," Barney said.

Perry was skeptical. "If they bloom in this climate." It was a dull and cloudy late afternoon, no warmth of the sun breaking through.

"Indeed." They were of the same mind.

Frankie was on edge about the plants too. She snapped at Perry when he started trying to repot them from the cardboard tubes they'd arrived in. "Leave those to me. If the roots get damaged, they'll die." She was as protective of her South American plants as Barney was of his grafts.

She went into the potting shed to set up pots with the precise soil combination she wanted. There was all sorts in there: perlite, sphagnum, blood and bone, any amount of sacks of specialist fertiliser, boric acid, guano. For all it was supposed to be organic it seemed like a chemical soup to Perry.

Barney rolled his eyes. "Don't worry about Frankie, she's just stressed. The shipping cost a fortune. But looking at them now, they're hardly going to be flying off the shelves, are they?"

Perry couldn't disagree. He was too tired to really care about Frankie or her plants either way. He'd done a morning at the Brewery and now he had to lug stone urns around the nursery. He was also worried that if he couldn't come up with anything at the Brewery he might not get his money. He'd be paid for his shifts, of course, but he was counting on some extra cash.

"I've got to go out, sort some things," Barney called to Frankie. "I probably won't be back until late. Might stop in at the pub on the way back."

"I won't wait up." Frankie was absorbed by her plants.

"I figured you wouldn't."

They were cool, Frankie and Barney. A solid couple but they didn't live in one another's pockets. Perry thought that if he ever settled down with someone it should be like that. Mind you, they worked together all hours. That would be enough to send most couples to the divorce courts.

But Barney was used to Frankie's moods, and in fairness, she was usually okay. Just not quite as laid back as Barney, for all she tried to kid herself that she was.

Perry wasn't sure if it might be awkward the next time he saw Priscilla down The Boatswain, but she was all friendliness, joking about the meat tray with Dilys.

"You ought to woo a girl with perfume, not meat," Dilys told him. It was useless to point out that he'd had no choice over what ticket came up when, but he knew Dilys was just teasing.

She seemed determined to play matchmaker, nudging them towards another date. "There's that Friday the Thirteenth film on at the cinema. You two ought to go. Friend of mine saw it, says it's worth a watch."

Perry felt put on the spot. "You working Saturday night?" he asked Priscilla, half hoping she was.

"Not this week, unless Ray swaps the shifts," she told him.

It was another date.

Later Dilys came and sat by him when Priscilla was out of earshot. "You're a nice looking lad, with those eyes, Perry. And you've got yourself a good situation owning your own boat. Don't you go letting Priscilla thinking she's granting you any favours."

Perry didn't have a response to this. He was saved from having to say something by Damon appearing.

"I asked for you about those shifts," he said. "Manager says to stop by on Tuesday."

Damon thanked him and Dilys looked typically curious. "You moving into a new line of work, Damon?"

Damon was breezy. "Just a bit of extra cash. Thinking of buying a car."

"Can't see you working with the Brewery boys in that get up." Dilys said what Perry was thinking. Damon was wearing a purple velvet frock coat, skin tight black jeans and winklepickers. He also had eyeliner on.

"Don't they give out overalls?" Damon asked.

They did in the brewing and bottling sections, because of hygiene requirements, but not in the warehouse. Perry was feeling uneasy about Tuesday. For

Mary's sake he didn't want the boys giving Damon a hard time. Damon had been to university, hadn't he? It seemed to Perry that something in an office would be more in Damon's line.

Dilys offered Damon a cigarette and he accepted. He was always scabbing Dilys's smokes: Perry rarely saw him reciprocate. Damon was always short of cash and Perry doubted he had any plans to buy a car. More likely he'd blow it all getting wasted.

It got Perry thinking though. He should probably get himself a driving licence at some point. There was more work you could do if you had a licence. For starters he'd be able to help Frankie and Barney out with deliveries. It had also been a slog getting to Swindon and back on public transport, and the possibility of one day getting his own wheels hung in his mind.

The following spring, nearly a year since he'd been released, Perry was old enough to drive. Although he hadn't got his licence, he joined a travelling carnival where he got to drive vans from time to time. Mainly he got to park them around the field once the rides had been set up.

He loved the fairground at first, the lights and the music, the candyfloss and the cheap stuffed toys won as prizes. He'd been to fairs as a kid with Jake, who used to make a killing lifting wallets in the crowds there.

Now Perry didn't have to pay for anything. It was unlimited free rides when he wasn't working. At the start it was like being given the keys to Disneyland. The gypsy kids who travelled with the fair all year round were blasé about it, but for the seasonal workers the novelty never quite wore off.

He and the other boys working there would also help hustle customers to the games. They'd be using the one rifle with straight sights, making it look easy. Then a punter would pay a couple of quid to have a go, and be handed a dodgy one.

Everything was rigged. Weighted cans, blunt darts, narrow hoops. "It's the fun of the game, not the win," Perry was told.

There was always plenty of food, mainly leftovers from the hotdog and burger stands. The fair folk would have resold much of it the next day rather than chuck it out, but the council health inspectors kept a sharp eye on things.

He discovered girls as well. Stevo, a swarthy, silver-tongued lad with a gold earring and a wheel tattooed on his upper arm, would pick the prettiest ones and Perry would pair off with their friends. It didn't usually get much further than a bit of fumbling behind the vans, as most of the girls would only go so far, but he felt like he was finally getting to be a man.

17

Fred came down to the canal around midday on Saturday. It had rained earlier in the morning but the sun was drying things off. The Emerald was looking bright, the dust washed off her paintwork by the rain.

"She's a fine boat, isn't she?" Fred was appreciative. It meant something to Perry, seeing the Emerald through Fred's eyes. She was indeed a beautiful vessel, all done up. A big contrast from the state he'd found her in several years ago.

Fred stepped onto the deck with the assuredness of someone who has been on boats before, and Perry showed him inside the cabin.

"She's not hooked up to power, but I get by. The motor needs replacing first. She can get up to the yard and back but for a longer voyage it's got to be fixed up."

Fred understood. "One project at a time. Some fine panelling you've got here." He tapped it admiringly.

Perry told him that much of it was original. "She wasn't in great shape when I found her, but there was still quite a bit that could be salvaged."

He gave Fred some of the story of how he had come across the Emerald and renovated her. Fred seemed fascinated. There was a wistful look in his eye as he thought about his own chances of taking to the waterways.

"How often do you have to refill the water?" Fred asked.

"Not more than every third week. With just me aboard and no washing machine, a full tank goes some way."

After he'd had a tour, Perry suggested they head to the Boatswain for a drink and some food. Mary did a good ploughman's on the weekend. Fred seemed very gratified to be asked.

"Plenty of boat people stop by there, do they?" he asked.

"Some do. A lot go to the White Stag," Perry said.

Fred knew of it. "Reputation for getting a bit rowdy, the Stag. Though they say there's a younger crowd in there these days."

The Boatswain was bustling with customers on a Saturday lunchtime. Perry was hoping he wouldn't be accosted by too many people he knew. Martin would be the most awkward if he showed up, as Perry didn't want Fred to rumble his motive for inviting him down to the boat. That said, Fred was a sound bloke and if Perry had just been working at the Brewery in the regular way of things, he might well have asked him over anyway.

Thinking about this made Perry feel better about it all. The whole information-gathering job still seemed uncomfortably close to police work.

"You worked at the Brewery long?" he asked Fred.

"Some years now. Not for many more, the way things are going now."

Fred's lugubriousness was going to make this easier for Perry.

"There's trouble there?" Perry asked.

Fred shrugged. "There's always something up. With the boss being knocked off it's anyone's guess what they'll do. New management always means changes, don't it?"

The meals arrived and Perry ordered more beers. He got Fred onto the subject of the Brewery's different beers, hoping that Fred would get another pint down him and loosen his lips some more. Fred didn't think much of any of Stantons' beers. He packed them onto the lorries and that was as much as he had to do with them. He'd have his birthday crate, no point throwing it out, but that was about it.

When Perry felt that Fred was becoming a bit more outspoken, he led the conversation on to Grover.

"That fellow who got sacked, nasty to think he might be a killer. Someone you worked alongside," Perry said.

"Grover? Never came as much of a surprise to me. I reckon the boss finally found out he was up to his neck in that labelling business," Fred said. "It's more puzzling that he lasted as long as he did."

"What labelling business?"

"It all got hushed up. Some scam they had going in the bottling section a few months back. They'd print extra Premium Gold labels and put them on the Stanton's Traditional and send it out for delivery. Well, it sells for a higher price, don't it? All muck if you ask me."

This must be it, Perry thought. "Management was doing that?"

"Oh no. Some of the boys in the plant, and a couple in the warehouse. I'd swear Grover was in on it, but he's a slippery one. Management had no idea what was going on for ages. The brown stuff hit the fan when they found out, you can be sure." Fred took an appreciative sip of his beer which was definitely not Stantons, Premium Gold or otherwise.

"Did they call in the coppers?"

Fred looked contemptuous. "No chance. Last thing they wanted was it all blown open, and customers finding out they'd been ripped off. Look very bad for the Brewery, that would. Because of that, some of them got away with a lot of money and kept their jobs, to stop them talking. Don't ask me how the scam worked with the invoicing, because it was all above my head, but they pulled it off alright."

Perry was wondering if Grover's counterfeiting skills might have come into play with the fake labels. He didn't really need to find out, and he certainly couldn't ask Fred. He had enough now to pass on to Martin. This would surely be the reason for the mysterious losses, with Arthur Stanton doubtless having cooked the books to conceal it all.

He'd thought that would be it, but Fred was on a roll now. The booze was making him voluble.

"It was some other business Grover got fired for. I can't say what, but he was up to something. Sometimes there at funny hours, outside of his shifts. Pilfering maybe, but nothing that got noticed. They're careful with all that, as you've seen."

Perry agreed that the stock control processes were rigorous.

"It all got tightened up after the labelling scam," Fred continued. "But there's always people looking for a way to make a little more on the side, isn't there? Me, I do my hours, take my pay and go home. We've got enough for our needs, Marge and I. Not worth the risk to get on the take, I always say."

"You reckon Grover did shoot Arthur Stanton?" Perry asked.

"Who's to say? If you'd asked me before it happened I'd have said no way, never the type. But now they've found those bullets at his place and he's scarpered, things don't look too good for him, do they?"

It wasn't a question that demanded an answer, but before Perry could have answered, Barney and Frankie Goodlock showed up. Perry was surprised to see them as he and Frankie usually opened the nursery all Saturdays.

Barney explained. "The irrigation system backed up again and flooded everywhere. It'll drain down by tomorrow, but we decided it was a good excuse for a break. You got two ploughman's left, Mary?" he called. Barney pulled up a chair and Frankie followed suit. Perry introduced them to Fred.

Perry and Fred had just about finished their lunches only Perry had left his pickled onion as usual. He'd gone off them ever since sharing a tent once with a lad who'd eaten a whole jar. Once he'd endured several hours of that proximity the onions had lost their appeal.

Barney, impatient for his own food, nicked Perry's neglected onion and ate it.

"Don't come near me tonight," Frankie told him. "You'll stink."

Barney just grinned. "Can't let it go to waste."

"Perry couldn't eat it," said Mary as she cleared their plates. "You're taking Priscilla out tonight, aren't you?"

You couldn't do anything without it becoming everyone's business, Perry thought. They were all such gossips.

Afterwards Perry walked with Fred back towards the canal as Fred headed homewards. "Familiar looking, that girl," he said.

"You've not drunk in the Boatswain before? She's always in there, of course." Perry couldn't think where else Fred might have bumped into Mary. The markets maybe?

Fred mulled over the suggestion. "It might be the markets, yes. It wasn't by the canal at any rate. It's been a good while since I was here."

Come harvest time Perry quit the carnival for seasonal work again since it paid better. He had grown sick of the gypsies that ran the carnival, constantly thieving, cheating and robbing. They did a big line in car radios.

The last thing Perry wanted was to be associated with all that again so he headed for the fields. This time he found work on a farm near the river. That was how he found the canal boat that was to become the Emerald.

On hot days, he and the other lads would head to the river to cool off after working in the fields. Perry couldn't remember when or where he had learned to swim, he just sort of managed it. Sometimes they swam races, mainly they just splashed around.

Her cabin leaking and in poor repair, they discovered the narrowboat moored under some willows. The trees had left a thick carpet of leaves through her broken roof and windows, which had all been smashed in. By a miracle she floated still and appeared otherwise seaworthy.

The others weren't interested in an old boat, once they realised she couldn't go anywhere. Perry however was taken by the vessel. He started by asking if he could clean her out to sleep on, and the farmer had no objection. The boat had belonged to an uncle who was long in a retirement home, his mind addled with age.

No one wanted her. She would have been left on the river to rot away and eventually sink without trace. But her kind of boat was built sturdy, built to last, so she'd withstood the last few years' neglect better than other craft might have done.

Under the dappled sunlight between the leaves that overhung the canal, Perry could on occasion get a glimpse of what she must have been. The bright colours she was once painted. The way the sun and the water would have reflected on her, like a floating jewel.

18

It wasn't the sort of film that you ended up getting romantic in. It was a full on horror film with people endlessly being stabbed. Perry put this down as to why he didn't really feel in the mood to try it on with Priscilla in the cinema.

She had looked nice again when they met outside. There was a big crowd milling around, queuing up for tickets since it was a popular film.

Perry bought the tickets and offered Priscilla popcorn but she declined. He chose seats more or less in the middle of the cinema and regretted this afterwards, since perhaps for a date it would have been more private to sit on the edge or at the back.

It didn't help that there were kids sitting in the rows behind them paying no attention to the screen. Perry could hear them whispering and making slurping noises. "Not there, Jase!" "Stop, that Jase!" he heard a young girl with a strong local accent murmuring behind him. This went on for most of the film, interspersed with giggling. She clearly didn't need rescuing.

He put his hand on the armrest, bumping into Priscilla's arm. After some awkwardness he held her hand for a bit. She seemed fine with that, but then pulled it away to cover her face during a shocking moment, and then didn't return it. So Perry sat there and tried to watch the film and ignore the alternative drama going on behind him.

"Someone might see, Jase."

"No one's looking. It's dark in here, innit?"

More muffled squeals.

Perry wished they could have moved and sat somewhere else. But Priscilla appeared absorbed with the action on screen so he didn't say anything.

Afterwards he mentioned stopping in a nearby bar but Priscilla had other ideas. "Why don't we go back to your boat for a drink?" she suggested.

"I've only got beer." She wasn't a beer drinker, he knew.

Priscilla turned to him and gave him a smile. "It's not going to matter what the drink is, Perry."

Surprised and also conflicted, he walked back with her to the canal and along the towpath. She stumbled once and he caught her, and she looked at him laughing, smiling up at him. She paused there for a moment so he said, "Are you alright?" and then she stood back and they started walking again. Afterwards he wondered if she wanted him to kiss her.

"Wasn't bad, was it?" he said of the film, not knowing what else to say.

"When she was stabbed on the raft it gave me a turn," Priscilla said. "Nasty, that was."

"Hope it won't give you nightmares."

She gave him another smile. "It might, if I'm all by myself."

Her meaning was quite clear which meant Perry, who really hadn't given much thought to something happening that night, now had to worry about the state of the Emerald.

When he arrived there, he had something quite different to worry about. Rose was there, sitting on the deck.

"What are you doing here Rosie? It's late." It was actually dusk, being this time of the year, but still. She should have been safely home with Ray and Mary.

"I took a walk. Thought I'd drop by," Rose said.

Priscilla was irritated. "You can't just impose on people all hours of the night. Mary will be wondering where you are."

Rose looked sulky. "Mary's not there. She went out."

"She's probably downstairs in the pub, and now she'll be worried about you."

"She's out-out. She often goes out at night when it's Ray on the bar."

This was news to Perry. Not that he kept track of Mary's movements. "Either way, you should go back, Rosie. It'll be long past your bedtime."

She was offended. "I'm a not a little kid."

"You're not an adult though," Priscilla pointed out. "And you're supposed to be with staying with Mary. What would those social services people say if they knew you were roaming around by yourself at all hours? They'd probably put you in a home, that's what."

Now Rose looked scared. Perry felt bad for her, thinking that Priscilla had gone a bit far. "It'll be alright, Rosie," he said. "You just run along now and no one will be any the wiser."

"I can't go back by myself now, it's dark. I'd be scared."

Perry didn't believe this but he could hardly force her to walk back alone past a place where a body had been found just a couple of weeks ago. "I'll have to walk her back," he said to Priscilla. "Do you want to come too, or wait here?"

Priscilla looked annoyed. The mood was spoilt for her. "I think I might call it a night, Perry. We'll catch up some other time."

It really wasn't his night. Priscilla walked off in the other direction and Perry reluctantly escorted Rose back. He didn't speak to her as he did so, but he also realised he wasn't as furious about it all as he might have been. In some ways it was all a bit of a relief.

Perry was working on the Emerald the next morning when Rose appeared again. He was fixing some leaks around a couple of the windows with sealant. It had rained in the night and some water had seeped through.

"Morning, Perry Beck," she greeted him.

"Morning."

She came and sat down on the side of the deck. "You dating that Priscilla then?" she asked.

"Maybe."

"She's not as a nice as Mary."

Perry used a cloth to rub off the excess sealant, having finished the bottom of one frame. "Mary's got a husband. Ray, if you hadn't forgotten." Mary was also a good bit older than him, though perhaps that kind of situation didn't matter once you got to a certain age.

"Not a nice husband, though."

Perry stopped what he was doing and looked at her. "Now Rosie Stanton, why would you say a thing like that? They've taken you in, Ray and Mary. You ought to be grateful."

Rose looked uncomfortable. "I am, truly. But even if he's okay with me he's not with her. Away from the bar he's different. They're always rowing. He says horrible things to her."

This surprised Perry but he didn't feel Rose should be airing the couple's dirty laundry in public. He said as much, and Rose got puzzled and thought he meant actual laundry. "They do that at the pub, they hang it on the line out the back. People can't help but see it if they walk past that way."

"That's not what I meant. I meant you shouldn't spread bad things about them."

The chin tilted up at this and defiant Rose returned. "It's not about them, it's about him. And it's all true."

"Sometimes grown-ups argue, Rose. It's just a thing. It blows over."

"You don't believe me, because you haven't heard it. You never believe me." She threw the accusation out and he knew what she was referring to.

He changed the subject. "You had Mary very worried last night."

Now she looked remorseful. "I didn't mean to worry her."

"You know it's not safe, given what happened to your dad. And your stepmum. There's funny people out there." There had been some concern raised about Rose's own safety given what had happened to her father and stepmother, but the police hadn't thought Grover, or whoever else might have shot them, would be interested in coming after the kid.

Perry saw tears in her eyes and felt guilty for scaring her. He handed her a bucket and a rag. "You can wipe down the deck if you like."

Rose brightened again. She was always happy to be given some task where she felt useful. In her usual way she started chattering and questioning him. Perry was used to working in silence but he could put up with it coming from her. Sometimes he'd tell her tales from his own boyhood though he had to leave a lot out. The darker stuff stayed buried.

"I know your mum's dead, but what about your dad?" she asked.

"I never had a dad."

"But you must have had a dad. Your mum couldn't have just had you," Rose persisted.

Perry started applying sealant to another window. "I mean I never knew him. Never met him. Don't even know his name."

"But he might be out there. Aren't you curious who he is?" She stopped wiping the deck and sat on the edge. "Both mine are dead. If I had one of them out there, I'd want to know."

Over the years Perry had once or twice wondered about his origins. He had a suspicion that the knowledge might be less pleasant than not knowing. He couldn't really explain this to Rose.

"You can't always find someone, even if you want to."

"Becky Pollard gets to find out who her real parents are when she's eighteen. She's adopted," Rose told him.

"That's different. When you're adopted, there are records." Not when you were abandoned though. How would you get hold of your birth certificate, he wondered. He'd never seen his. Might the social services people have it? Or had someone such as Black Bessie ever seen it?

Then he stopped this train of thought because it would lead to no good.

Most of the permanent farm labourers had homes nearby, and the seasonals had families they could return to. Perry had no one.

This might have been why he'd felt a hankering after something of his own. Something more permanent. He'd had a couple of brief tastes of that in foster homes and got wondering what it would be like to live in the same place for years, not always moving on or being moved on. Thinking about this sowed the seeds of the great idea that took root in Perry.

People spoke of a "roving spirit" and some of the seasonals had it in their bones. They liked the constant change and sought it out.

"You reckon you'll be here next spring, Tom?"

"No, I'll be going Sussex way. Lovely part of the country they say."

One time Perry was offered the chance to join an itinerant rug sale. The workers travelled from place to place, staying in cheap digs and seeing the sights when they got time off. The work was endlessly rolling and loading and unrolling carpets off a lorry and dragging them about warehouses.

The girl who asked him had a liking for him, but Perry hadn't realised this at the time when he declined the job. He was always oblivious to female interest in him. His background wasn't a thing to recommend him, he had no money and no apparent prospects. He also lacked the glib charm and devil-may-care attitude of the blokes that seemed to score well with women.

Despite this he was content enough. He wasn't even eighteen yet so there was plenty of time for all that. For now he had other priorities than settling down with a girl. He had no home and there was a boat with no owner, a vacant cabin. Could it be made liveable again?

At this stage he wasn't thinking any further than just having a fixed roof over his head that was his and his alone.

19

Things didn't indeed look too good for George Grover when police fished him out of a well a week later.

Children playing outside some ruined farm buildings on the outskirts of Bath had discovered an old well. They couldn't see water in it because it was too far down, but it stank. One of them threw up at the stench. They ran back telling their parents how awful it was.

"It's worse than Sam's farts. Worse than that rotten egg you cracked open." "It's like the devil's dog-doo. Couldn't stand near it without wanting to puke."

At first it was presumed that a farm animal had fallen down there. But a woman in the area had gone missing and it was on the news that night. One of the parents notified the police. Just in case. You couldn't be too careful, these days.

Avon and Somerset Constabulary went to investigate, and instead of a woman or a rotting sheep, fished out Grover.

According to an autopsy he'd been down there for a good couple of weeks but it was impossible to ascertain the date of death any more precisely from the medical evidence. The details of what happened to a waterlogged body semi-immersed in water of a specific pH made some good and grisly reading for those of a morbid mindset.

It was no accident or suicide: George Grover had been shot in the back of the head. And from what the police could establish, he had been shot with the same weapon as the Stanton murders. So it became headline news once again, with Rose's father's and stepmother's photos splashed all over the front pages once more.

"Triple Murder: Corpse Found in Well" "Murder Suspect Found Shot" "Brewery Murders: Mystery Thickens".

Mary and Dilys tried to protect Rose, but the posters were outside all the newsagents. Like everyone else Rose had got it into her head that Grover had done it, and that it was only a matter of time before the police caught up with him. It had made it easier for her, thinking that the case was essentially solved.

Now it was all blown open once again. The police were all over the brewery, interviewing all the same people they had done with the earlier murders. They were still getting nowhere. Perry was relieved he'd finished his work there since he didn't fall under their radar. He'd started long after Grover had been fired, and left before Grover had turned up dead. There was nothing to connect him to any of it so the police didn't think to question him. Not that he could have told them much anyway.

Mary took the line that Grover was still the guilty party and it was all a "gangland killing". "He did your parents in, Rose, and then someone did him in. He was a bad man and that's what happens to bad men."

Whether Mary actually believed this or was just saying it to ease Rose's fears, she never admitted. Dilys was of an entirely different mind. "I never thought it was that Grover fellow. Looked too obvious, didn't it? Those bullets found at his place were a clear fit up. And why would he be hanging around looking for work when he could have gone on the run?"

"Maybe he needed to wait around to do Sybil in?" Mary suggested.

"Why would he even want to do her in?" Priscilla wondered.

Dilys had elaborate theories on this. "A sex crime, most probably. He had an obsession about her and Arthur Stanton found out and warned him off so he shot him. Maybe they were having an affair. Or maybe Sybil rejected his advances so Grover took the gun to her as well."

Perry, who had seen Sybil, thought such an obsession unlikely. "That doesn't explain why someone shot Grover, though."

"Maybe she had another lover? And he got mad at Grover."

It all seemed very implausible but who really knew anything?

"What happens to a body down a well?" Priscilla asked. "Does it all swell up?" She was always one for the grisly, Perry had noticed.

"They bloat, don't they?" Ray said. "All the gases inside. Then they float up again. That's why the mafia put them in concrete. Sink them and keep them down."

Priscilla shuddered, relishing the thought. "They didn't put him in concrete down the well, did they?"

"They probably didn't think anyone would find him too soon, stuck in the middle of nowhere," Ray pointed out.

Who "they" were remained a mystery. It was interesting to consider that they might be plural, since the police seemed fixed on a single perpetrator.

Martin privately speculated to Perry that it might all have something to do with the labelling scam he'd uncovered. Martin's uncle's client was satisfied now he finally knew what was going on and Perry had been well remunerated. The new engine was finally within his grasp.

Perry had told Martin everything he had discovered, though not necessarily where he had discovered it from. He had no desire to implicate Fred as any kind of grass. Nor did he wish his own association with King John and the Company to be known.

"If Grover had been some kind of kingpin, maybe Arthur was threatening to turn him in. Sybil also knew about it, let's say. So Grover had to kill both of them. Then one of the other blokes panicked and did Grover in. Maybe he'd made off with all the cash?"

The scam had had to be reported to the police due to the murder investigation. Perry understood why but he wasn't comfortable with it. He supposed it was none of his business after all. He'd been asked to do a job and he'd done it. Arthur Stanton's silent partner had been even less pleased. Now word was out about the labelling scam, and even though it was long resolved they'd had orders cancelled. The partner wanted to sell out of the whole business, Martin said, but now it was in choppy waters.

Another brewery worker who escaped questioning was Damon. As Perry feared, Mary's brother had been so useless that he'd barely lasted half a morning before the other blokes got fed up and sent him packing. Perry got this information from Fred, who had taken to passing by the Boatswain for a drop every now and then. Fred had caught the boating bug since his visit to the Emerald and liked to come down and spin a yarn with the river folk.

Even though his own desire to take to the water would have to remain a pipe dream, given his wife's antipathy to the idea.

"Pranced on down in some fancy get up, that Damon, and stood mooning about, barely able to lift an empty crate with two dozen balloons tied to it. Bit of a snoop too, if you ask me. Don't know if he thought there might be cash lying about the place," Fred had said to Perry.

No one ever seemed to manage much of a conversation with Damon. He was a bit of a mystery. Dilys had tried to draw him out once or twice, as she did with everyone, but had eventually given up. "I'd tell him to get off his backside if I was Mary," she said.

Martin had also suggested to Perry that there would be plenty more work if he had a mind to it. He assured Perry that if anything, it would likely be on the opposite side to the police. Martin wanted to focus on criminal law rather than the conveyancing work that his uncle specialised in, and inquiry agents were a vital part of the process.

"Surveillance, process serving, there's a tonne of work out there. Lucrative too, depending on the job. You could pick and choose what you wanted to do."

Martin was waiting on his law exam results after which he had to do some legal course in London, followed by a couple of years apprenticeship. It sounded like a long haul to Perry but he admired Martin for his dedication.

It wouldn't hurt to do more work for Harcourts, Perry supposed. He felt he could trust both Martin and Jeff Harcourt. He'd definitely mull it over.

He'd never been afraid of trying a new line of work. Once Perry had got the green light to clear up the boat and sleep on her, she became his project. Every spare hour he had, every extra penny he could earn he used to fix the boat up so she could at least be inhabited.

"You playing Swallows and Amazons?" one of the other farm labourers asked him, but Perry didn't get the reference. They laughed at his efforts, preferring the dry sheds and hay bales to a leaky hut on the water.

The farmer had no use for an old narrowboat and the craft wasn't worth much to anyone in the state she was in. Perry went into town and looked up prices in a boating magazine in the newsagent. He was surprised that they weren't as high as they might be, though still out of his league for now.

He was determined to save up and buy the boat. He could put a time on when this idea had come to him, from simply doing up the boat to actually owning her. But once he had the notion, he was fixed on it. He went and opened himself a bank account with the few quid he had, and started putting everything into it.

He took on extra work. Whatever someone needed doing, he'd do it if he could. He rarely went to the pub or the pictures with the others. He got a reputation for being tight-fisted but he didn't care. He had a goal and he committed everything to it.

20

Perry never forgot the day that everything changed. It stood as a clear divider between past and present.

A day ago it had seemed like an endless summer, as though everything could drift along for always. Hot day after hot day, a hard few hours of labour, a cool drink and the camaraderie of the regular crowd. Back to the boat and the peace of the river. Perry had never felt quite so settled.

At the back of his mind it nagged him. Should he be moving on? Something about his early upbringing and life had given him the sense that to stick in one spot too long was unsafe. Even if he moved a couple of miles up the canal it would be a change.

He pondered it from time to time, sitting on the Emerald, tying flies or just basking in the late sun with a beer. He spent less time in the Boatswain, having lost interest in Priscilla. Since Rose had said what she'd said about Ray and Mary, Perry had also felt a sense of unease about the pub. He liked Mary and he had liked Ray. As much as he wanted to dismiss it all as a silly kid's imagination, he wasn't so sure he could. Something resonated. So while he still put in the odd hour of labour, he avoided the place at other times.

Dilys noticed he was out of sorts. Few things escaped her.

"You alright, Perry?" she asked when he finally stopped by for a drink one evening.

"Not so bad," he said.

"You had a falling out with Priscilla?" Dilys asked.

Perry shrugged. "Not so I'm aware of. Just been busy with the boat." Dilys might or might not buy this. He didn't really care.

And then everything was turned upside down.

The day came that the police paid a visit to Ray and Mary. It was such a small, simple thing. A telephone record. A single call made from the Boatswain to the lodgings of George Grover, some weeks before he became the late George Grover.

The police, who had been concentrating their lines of inquiry on the Brewery, now had a connection to somewhere else.

Both Mary and Ray claimed never to have met George Grover. "He may have come in the pub, but I don't recognise every face," Ray said. "We get a lot just passing through what with the river traffic."

The police wanted to know who had been working that day, whether the public were ever allowed to make calls, and an endless amount of things. The phone was located behind the bar and was a regular private phone, not a payphone.

"We'd notice if someone went to use it. Even one of the regulars, and I don't remember any of them asking. If anyone needs a taxi we usually call for them," Mary said.

Then they worked out what the date of the phone call had been. The Saturday of the beer dispenser fit out, and the barbecue.

"That's obvious then, it was one of their workmen," the police were told. But they checked with the firm: they'd long packed up and gone by two o'clock. The call had been made at two thirty. All the workers had alibis. None of the barbecue attendees did, except from one another.

Pretty much everyone had gone through the back door at some point to use the facilities. To reach these they would pass along a narrow hallway past the stairs that led up to the living quarters. At the end of the doorway an interior door led through to the main room of the bar, where the phone was. This interior door, usually locked when the pub was open, had been left open on the day of the barbecue for people's convenience. So people could use the public lavatory rather than Ray's and Mary's private bathroom upstairs, they explained to the police.

The phone would have been fully accessible to anyone entering the bar.

Fingerprints were no use given the time that had passed. It was only covered with Ray's and Mary's.

"Making a phone call hardly proves you did a murder," Martin said. "It's only circumstantial evidence."

But it was odd. For someone to have known Grover well enough to phone him in his lodgings, and never disclose that they knew him given everything that had happened, it was odd.

"Could it have been a wrong number?" Mary asked the police. "Maybe it's similar to a taxi firm?" Not that anyone had called a taxi firm that day, but she couldn't think what else to suggest.

But it wasn't similar to any taxi firm or any other number the police were aware of. They had also established that the following day, the Sunday, was the last day that George Grover had been seen. A neighbour, coming back from a dog walk, had seen Grover driving out the following morning in his clapped out old Volvo. The car had been located, abandoned, outside an old warehouse near Bath. Just few miles from the well where the body had been found. The only fingerprints on the car were Grover's.

The police officer leading the investigation was a Detective Inspector Paul Oak. DI Oak was around thirty and had the sort of looks that saw Priscilla rushing to touch up her make up whenever he stopped by. Dilys tried to be dismissive but Perry noticed she was also wearing more lipstick than usual.

Everyone was under suspicion. Everyone got questioned.

For Perry, it gave him horrible flashbacks. Even though he wasn't officially being arrested, just "helping the police with their inquiries", he insisted on having a solicitor present. At the back of his mind was Old Owen's dry voice: "Always demand a brief, son. Don't you open your mouth unless you've got a brief there."

DI Oak was bemused by Perry's request because no one else had made such a demand. The police were only gathering initial witness statements to try to piece together who had been at the barbecue when, and what had gone on. But Perry was legally entitled to make the request.

Perry, who had assumed that Martin could sit in with him as a favour, was disconcerted to find that Martin wasn't yet qualified to do so. It would have to be Jeff Harcourt and Perry didn't have the funds to pay him.

Martin's uncle was aware that Perry might face some stickier questioning later on due to the Brewery investigation job he'd undertaken. With this in mind he was prepared to help out pro bono. Given the time the police were taking to identify a suspect, he didn't want Perry fitted up for it.

Perry made his statement. They had all drunk a fair amount at the barbecue which left his memory hazy. He remembered Ray's friend, Frankie, Dilys and Martin all entering the pub at some point. He had also done so himself. He couldn't remember the others entering, but that wasn't to say they hadn't. Remembering the order of it was harder. He also hadn't been looking at his watch.

"Big Trev would have been first, after that it's anyone's guess," he said.

The whole process didn't take long but there was mention of "follow up questioning". They weren't going to be off the hook for a while.

Two days later Perry was asked in for questioning again. This time the police had done their homework and had been through their file on him.

"Got a bit of form, haven't you, Mr Beck?" This interviewer was a ginger haired cop with a scrubby looking moustache. He reminded Perry of a weasel.

Fortunately Perry had Jeff Harcourt with him again. "I think you'll find that my client had one single conviction as a juvenile, which is now spent."

DI Oak was looking at the notes in the file. "Long sentence for a first offence, wasn't it? 'Weapon present on entry' - a gun, was it?"

"A penknife." This would be in the court transcripts if they checked.

DI Oak frowned. "A penknife?" He checked through again. "Ah, it was Justice Peters. You lucked out there, Mr Beck."

Perry looked at Jeff Harcourt who explained. "The judge isn't known for his leniency."

"Indeed." The ginger weasel fixed his eye on Perry. "So you've been doing a bit of labouring here and there, and all of a sudden you show up at Stanton's."

Jeff Harcourt explained the reason for Perry working at the brewery.

"Very convenient, that," the ginger one said. "Gave you a nice excuse to go poking around, didn't it?" Perry could just about bear Oak but this weasel was beyond the pale.

"You don't have to answer that, Perry," Jeff Harcourt reminded him. Perry remained silent. He hated everything about the interview room. The sickly light, the smell of stale coffee in polystyrene cups. The plastic chairs. The table with the tape recorder sitting there like a bomb. It brought memories back that he'd tried for years to bury.

"And then when you found out about this funny business, you chose not to inform the police. Even though a serious fraud had been perpetrated."

"I wasn't hired by the police," Perry said.

"So if there was money involved, you'd choose not to do your civic duty?"

Jeff Harcourt objected.

"We're not in a court of law, Mr Harcourt," the ginger weasel pointed out. "Your client hasn't even been charged. We're just trying to get to the bottom of this. Basic information, that's all."

He consulted Perry's background file. "Ever handled a gun, Mr Beck?"

Perry shifted in his seat. He thought of the dodgy air rifles at the fairground. But the police wouldn't necessarily know about his time there. Then there had been a time on one of the farms where they'd picked up an old shotgun they found in a shed and played around with it. It had no bullets and the trigger was broken. But no one would know about that either. Both instances were meaningless but he was aware how they could twist things. It took a few words to turn *"once helped out on the shoot-the-ducks stall at Tranter's Fair"* into *"spent his youth obsessed with handling guns"*.

"No."

"Had you ever met George Grover?"

Perry couldn't lie about this, since he'd mentioned it to the others and Frankie had also been there. "I saw him once."

"And where was this?" DI Oak was making notes, though the tape recorder was still rolling.

"Goodlock Nursery. I turned up for work and he was just leaving."

The two officers exchanged a glance. "How did you know who he was?" DI Oak asked.

"Frankie mentioned it. Said he'd been looking for work." Perry assumed they would know who Frankie was by now.

"What about Arthur Stanton, had you ever met him?" ginger asked.

"No." He'd obviously met the daughter but he wasn't going to offer that unless they asked. They'd know anyway, given Rose had been living at the pub.

DI Oak picked up the questioning. "Do you know of anyone who had a grudge against George Grover?"

Another no. He hadn't been liked down the Brewery, but Perry would be damned if he'd drop Fred in it.

"Do you know of anyone who had a grudge against Arthur Stanton? I imagine he was known in the area. Supplied beer to the Boatswain, didn't he? Or what about his wife? Anyone with a grudge against her?"

Only Rose, Perry thought. She'd hated her stepmother. He was even more damned if was going to mention that.

DI Oak perceived that he was getting less and less out of Perry. He also didn't see any real motive. It would have been convenient if the one party present with a record turned out to be the key suspect, but right now he couldn't see it. He tried a different tactic. "You live on the canal, don't you?"

Was it a trick question? They knew he lived there, they'd sent officers round there before. He didn't answer.

"Must be quite a nice life, living on a boat," DI Oak said. "Easy to sail off if you get sick of a place."

"I suppose."

Jeff Harcourt interrupted. "If you've finished questioning my client about the shootings..."

"Just a moment." DI Oak got to his point. "Have any of the other river folk moved off recently? The permanents, not the leisure boaters. Liveaboards they call you, don't they?"

Perry shrugged. He couldn't think of anyone, nor would he mention it if he had.

DI Oak continued. "Quite a few of the river folk frequent the Boatswain, I'd imagine?"

Again, it was something they must already know. "A few," Perry said.

"Perhaps they'll have noticed any recent disappearances. We'll ask down there." DI Oak wrapped up the interview. If he'd expected to get anything out of

Perry, he'd failed. But Perry sensed the detective was smarter than he looked.

It was a good life on the boat, even when she was in poor repair and unable to move. Once he'd fixed up the cabin so it no longer leaked, and cleaned it out, the narrowboat offered a surprising amount of space. Like a whole house, really. He found out later that she was considered a smaller boat but to Perry she seemed like a palace.

Most of the woodwork turned out to be intact. What needed replacing were all the broken windows. He'd boarded them up as a temporary measure, but he used a little of his money to get glass for a couple of them. That way he at least had some light.

He didn't want to make the boat look too smart. He was shrewd enough to realise that the farmer might put on a higher price if he thought he could get away with it.

Perry stored up bits and pieces of this and that, knowing they'd come in useful later on. Lumber, spare nails. Strictly speaking some of it wasn't his to take but he figured nails left rusting on the floor of a shed were just going to waste.

Tools were a problem. He knew how to use them, thanks to a carpentry course when he'd been inside. But they were expensive and he was still nowhere near to buying the boat. He figured since it was still the farmer's boat, he could borrow some of the farm tools to work on it.

It gave his life a sort of structure that it hadn't had before. Previously he'd just been getting by, just existing. Not working towards anything. There wasn't any sense of a future, just each day as it came, the next day much like the previous.

And yet all along he had felt he should be building towards something. Now he was. It was about owning a boat, a place of his own to live on. He couldn't say what was beyond that. It was too far to guess and he didn't want to jinx it by getting his hopes up. But if he pulled it off, it would open up more opportunities.

21

It was the thing about convictions. They weren't ever really spent because the police kept the records regardless. It was the taint that King John had warned of. Perry was tainted. No matter what he did, or where he went, he was someone who had spent over six months in juvenile detention.

"I didn't know you'd been in trouble with the law," Mary said to him when she served him a beer. She looked anxious.

Perry first thought she was worried about having a convicted criminal in the pub. Then he realised she was worried for him, because he was under greater scrutiny than the others as a result.

"It was a while ago," he told her.

"How old were you?"

"Fourteen," Perry said. It seemed a lifetime ago.

Mary was surprised. "You would have just been a kid! They can't be coming at you for that, years later. Talk about give a dog a bad name and hang him. And nothing since?"

Perry shook his head.

"Surely it all gets sealed off at some point, then?"

"Yes, but the coppers always have it in their files."

Mary was feeling a sense of misplaced guilt on Perry's behalf because the phone call had been made from her premises, and he had only been there at her invitation. She felt this to a varying extent on behalf of all of the barbecue attendees and had mentioned it to Ray, who had told her not to be so damn silly.

Ray reckoned he was the only one who shouldn't be under suspicion. He had overseen the barbecue for the first half and been sat on a deckchair for the second half. He claimed he hadn't needed to take a leak. He made a point of mentioning this whenever the topic came up.

Mary opened some peanuts and tipped them into a bowl. She pushed them towards Perry. "On the house."

Martin was the only one who seemed energised by the whole affair. For him it was a fascinating glimpse of the other side of the fence, joining the band of "suspects". He had no real fears of anything actually being pinned on him since he had no motive, and alibis for the earlier shootings. It was all a bit of a game to him.

As such, Martin had decided to run his own informal investigation. He took a table at the Boatswain and insisted on going over the evidence with an eager Dilys and a reluctant Perry. Priscilla, also fascinated by it all since the police had gone relatively easy on her, hovered nearby whenever she got a chance.

The Boatswain was even busier these days thanks to the notoriety of it being "the Murder Pub". The regulars took it all with a grain of salt and had no desire to find another drinking spot. And for every casual visitor who thought it might be wiser to try another establishment, there were a dozen nosey parkers attracted by the pub's notoriety.

Therefore Priscilla, to her annoyance, was run off her feet. Mary had even dragged the useless Damon down to clear glasses. He ambled about, a glazed look in his eye, so far managing not to break any.

"We've got three dates to focus on," Martin said. "There's the night Arthur Stanton was killed. Then there's the night that Sybil was shot. And then the afternoon of the barbecue, when the phone call was made."

Dilys tapped Martin's notepad with the cigarette she had just drawn out of a packet. "That's easy, when she was shot. We were all here, weren't we? Mary and Ray had a lock-in."

"Those two fellows that Ray knows weren't here that night," Priscilla, passing by, pointed out.

Martin added them to his list. He had drawn three columns: motive, means and opportunity.

Arthur Stanton's death was the tricky one because it had happened around midnight when everyone was supposedly asleep. "That rules me out," Mary said, "since I was here with Ray." She had come to sit with them, letting Priscilla manage the bar. Mary looked tired. Her face was paler than usual and drawn. No wonder, given all the drama at her pub.

"Unless one of you was fast asleep and the one woke up." Dilys was starting to enjoy this, though she didn't seriously believe that Mary or Ray had had anything to do with it. The phone call from their own pub was too obvious for starters.

"I sleep like a log," Mary said. "And thank God I do, with Ray's snoring.

"More your luck, Mary." Barney Goodlock had just dropped by with Frankie. "I wake up if a leaf falls." He pulled up a chair, looking bronzed and healthy. He had spent the day working outside without a hat and had caught the sun.

"It's getting to sleep that's more of an issue," Mary continued. "If I close up the pub and he's already gone to bed, by the time I'm there he's like a foghorn."

Perry caught something in Mary's expression when she said this. As though she were trying to say it jokingly, but more resentment seeped through than she had intended. He couldn't blame her for getting mad with Ray over it. Sleep deprivation did odd things to a person.

"Perry got a grilling," Dilys told Barney. News of Perry's interrogation had spread, thanks to Martin

Barney frowned. "They can't seriously suspect Perry? He didn't even know any of them. Not that any of us did."

"And he was here with all of us for the lock-in," Dilys said. "Though locks don't mean much to you, do they Perry? You might easily have slipped in and out. Not saying you did, but it's probably crossed the police's minds."

Frankie placed her and Barney's drinks on the table. "I'm glad today's over," she said. "Too long, too hard, too hot."

They returned to Martin's notes and the problem of the barbecue versus the lock-in. How every single person at the barbecue had been in the lock-in the night of Sybil's death. Save for those with the key - Mary and Ray - or Perry with his lock pickling skills, the others couldn't have done it.

Yet nearly everyone at the barbecue could have made the phone call.

Frankie looked at the table of names, times and other details that Martin had drawn up. "Very methodical, aren't you?" She put it back down and picked up her cider. "It seems to me that they're making an awful lot out of a single phone call. Besides, someone might have come in the front way while we were all out the back frying sausages."

"I locked the front door after the workmen left," Mary said. "It was only the inner door that was open. Anyone getting in would have had to go by the back door, so we would have seen them."

"What time did you end that lock-up, then?" Dilys asked. "I was so blotto I couldn't tell my arse from my elbow. If a line of dancing bears had come through the window I wouldn't have noticed."

"You don't remember getting off with Big Trev then? Dancing on a table with your skirt over your head?" Barney grinned.

"Give over."

Martin drummed his pen against the notebook. "I can't see how it was done. Maybe we're missing something but it all seems like a wild goose chase to me."

The night of Arthur Stanton's death they had all been in their separate places. The night of Sybil's murder they had all been inside the Boatswain drinking. The afternoon of the phone call they had all been outside the Boatswain. Perry thought it seemed like a pattern, but did it hold any significance?

"I wonder why the phone call had to be made then," he said. It was the first thing he'd said at all so everyone stopped and looked at him. He felt awkward. "I mean if it was a risky thing, to make a call that might be traced, why make it then? Anyone might have passed by and seen you making the phone call."

They thought about this for a few moments, one or two people darting glances at one another. It was an odd thing, having a seed of suspicion sown in an otherwise friendly group.

"It suggests it was urgent. Perhaps Grover was only available at certain times?" Martin suggested.

Barney stood up. "I can't do this. Like it's a game, when the chances are that someone at the barbecue did make that call but won't own up to it. It gives me the creeps. Let the police handle it."

There were a few shameful glances. Frankie looked unruffled by her husband walking off. Mary also excused herself and went back behind the bar to serve some customers who had just come in. As soon as she did so, Priscilla darted back to the conversation. "You make any progress?" she asked.

"I think we're calling it a day." Martin closed the notepad and laid his biro on top of it. "For now at least."

He wasn't going to let it go, Perry thought. He recognised the gleam of determination in Martin's eye. He was tenacious, Perry would give him that.

When trying to raise the money for the boat, the one thing that Perry could have made some quick cash with were his lock picking skills. He'd found out what locksmiths charged for a callout when someone lost their keys, and it blew his mind. But due to his record, he couldn't get a license as a locksmith.

He could have done some casual work but he didn't want the others to know about his art. As soon as they did they'd start suspecting him of everything. Anything that went missing, he'd be blamed for. People didn't like thinking they weren't secure in their own homes.

So he stayed on at the farm for as long as there was work, living aboard the narrowboat. Even through winter when it was freezing. The farmer didn't mind him continuing to live there, it was no skin off his nose. Some days it seemed like an impossible dream to own it and get it moving again, but Perry never gave up.

Later on he found some work on a nearby pig farm run by a friendly couple. They even offered to let him lodge with them but Perry was reluctant to leave the narrowboat. With most of the windows boarded up she wasn't badly insulated, he'd plugged any gaps and draughts with what he could, and he had plenty of blankets.

The boat had no real facilities though. It was like camping. He had meals with the piggery couple and washed himself and his clothes there.

He even had Christmas with them, and it was the best he'd had since the early days with The Company. All the food and the warmth. A real log fire. He even got presents: the farmer's wife had knitted him a jumper and they gave him a Christmas bonus in cash. Every little bit helped.

22

Detective Inspector Paul Oak also seemed interested in doors and windows when he visited the Boatswain next day. He asked Mary and Ray over and over again about the state of various locks and latches. His sergeant, not the ginger weasel but a stolid local man, poked around outside and sat in the police car using the radio.

DI Oak went looking over the windowsills and doorway, making marks in his little black notebook. With Ray's permission - not that he could have denied it - Oak also looked around out the back and upstairs. The police had already been through the place with a fine tooth comb the previous day and nothing had been changed. So what he expected to find or what he thought he had missed was anyone's guess.

Priscilla was only too thrilled to see him. She rushed out the back, sprayed on a perfume sample she had in her bag, and plumped up her lips with some gloss. She wasn't working that day but had stopped by to pick up her wages.

"You're here for the customers, not the policeman's ball," Mary said.

"I'm not rostered on and we're not even open, are we? Is there really such a thing as a policeman's ball?" Priscilla asked.

"Why don't you invite yourself along to it and find out?" Mary returned to polishing some of the optics.

Perry was only there because Ray had gone off somewhere and now Mary had something with her back and couldn't lift anything. She had been acting funny lately. He couldn't put his finger on what it was. Once or twice her eyes had looked red and Perry felt a sense of unease as he remembered Rose's claims.

It had made him look differently at Ray, even though he had been inclined to dismiss it all. Ray was something of a bully. His jovial air and "jostling" with people, as he liked to call it, could have a mean edge. Maybe Mary did cop it worse when the two of them were alone.

Mary put the cloth she had been using on the optics behind the bar. "Can I get you a drink?" she asked Oak.

"None of the strong stuff, since we're on duty. A cup of tea would be great if you've got it."

"How about your sergeant?" Mary asked.

"He'll have white with two sugars, thanks. White with none for me."

DI Oak was the last person Perry wanted to bump into after the interrogation the police had put him through. Even if the ginger one had been worse, they were all cops and as bad as each other. It irked Perry to see Priscilla fluttering her eyelashes at Oak, even if Perry himself had lost interest in her.

After all, it was Perry who had broken it off. Priscilla had suggested another outing but Perry had declined on account of some stuff he had to do with the boat. He hadn't suggested a future time. Priscilla liked Perry but considered that there were other fish in the sea, so cut her losses and cast her net elsewhere. DI Oak was her current quarry.

Perry kept his head down and returned to the cellar as quickly as he could after bringing up each crate. What with Mary and Ray and their respective back problems, the fridges badly needed restocking. They should get into a different game, Perry thought.

Rose was in the main bar, sitting at a table reading a comic. Even after they opened it was generally quiet at this time of day, so no one was bothered about her being there. She knew DI Oak quite well by now, as he had been heading the investigation ever since her father had been killed.

"Alright Rose?" Paul Oak said to her as he went past. "You keeping well?"

Rose looked up at him warily. At least she wasn't affected by his charms, Perry thought. He found he resented the detective inspector's easy ways with everyone. He supposed Oak had a job to do, but he wished he'd go and do it somewhere else. Perry slunk back to the cellar, thinking to stay down there until the DI had gone.

Instead, Oak joined him in the cellar. "Tidy set up down here," he said. It was well organised. Ray was a freak for order and there had been a big clear out when the new dispensing system had been installed.

Perry ignored him and added the empty crate he was carrying to a stack.

"Anything in the way of exits around here?"

Perry looked around the small, windowless room. What was Oak expecting? A trapdoor or a secret panel? Neither was likely, since the cellar had been dug long after the pub had been built. Something to do with the proximity to the water and the chances of flooding and culverts. Ray had spoken of it once but Perry couldn't remember the specifics.

"There's a drain." He indicated a round opening about six inches in diameter, covered by an iron grille.

"Not much chance of exiting through that, is there?" DI Oak said, making another note in his black book. He looked back up at Perry. "One of John Lochinvar's boys, weren't you? Not that we're interested in any of that now," he added hastily, seeing Perry start. "It was years ago, I know. He's something of a legend in these parts."

Never trust them, Perry thought. The scuffers were interested in one thing, and that was fitting you up whether you'd done it or you hadn't. King John's words rang in his ears.

"You should never have got eighteen months, for a first offence, at that age. It was well before my time, but still. There are better guidelines now," DI Oak said.

Much good hearing any of this was to Perry. He had no idea why Oak was trying to ingratiate himself with him. If Oak had a notion that Perry might turn snitch, or that he had something to hide, he was sorely mistaken. Since those long ago days with the Company, Perry had gone straight and stayed straight.

Perry could hardly skulk about down in the cellar when it was obvious there was nothing more to do, so he followed DI Oak back upstairs into the pub.

A smiling Priscilla brought a mug of tea over to the detective inspector. But at that moment his sergeant came in and declined his cup. "Just had a call. We need to head out Banbury way."

"The usual?"

"The usual."

DI Oak turned to Priscilla. "Much as I hate to abandon a cup of tea, duty calls. I'll take a rain check if that's alright." His tone was friendly and polite but not in any way suggestive. He nodded to Mary and Perry as he left and said "bye, now" to Rose.

The two detectives exited, leaving Priscilla momentarily dejected. She quickly recovered her spirits. "He's alright, that Detective Oak, isn't he?" she said. The comment was directed to Mary.

"I can't see you as a copper's wife," Mary said, with uncharacteristic acid.

Priscilla flounced off, having no reason to stick around now she had her pay packet and DI Oak had gone.

After she left, it seemed to Perry that Mary suddenly snapped and went off at Rose for some mess that Rose had supposedly made somewhere. Rose fled out the back in tears and Mary rolled her eyes. Then she went off to the kitchen herself.

Dilys Jones, arriving for her shift which was only an hour that morning, caught the tail end of it.

"Something's up with Mary," Perry said by way of explanation.

"There's no prizes for guessing what's up with Mary," Dilys said. She went out to the kitchen to get the carpet sweeper. She came back, leant it against the wall, and sat down at the table Rose had vacated, gesturing for Perry to join her. "I'll have a quick cigarette before I start. Are those fresh teas on the bar?" On learning they were she took one and suggested Perry had the other.

He felt a resistance to drinking Oak's cast off beverages, though it sounded silly to say it. So he simply said he wasn't thirsty.

"So what is up with Mary?" Perry asked. He was worried about her, what with all Rose had said.

"In the club, isn't she?"

The bowling club? The nearby tennis club? Perry was at a loss.

"Up the duff. Bun in the oven. She's pregnant."

Perry didn't know what to say. He knew nothing about those kind of things. He looked at Dilys for clues. "That's good then, isn't it? Ray'll be pleased."

Dilys flicked her ash into the tray. "Hardly."

"Why not?" To Perry it seemed normal that a married couple would eventually have a kid and be glad about it.

"He can't have them, can he?" Dilys made a motion with two of her fingers. Perry appeared more and more confused. Dilys was amused by his bewilderment. "The snip. A vasectomy. No swimmers a'swimmin'."

"Then how's Mary expecting?"

Dilys laughed in exasperation. "It's not his. See? So it's someone else's, isn't it? And Ray doesn't know about any of it."

It was all well beyond Perry's pay grade. Yet he found himself a reluctant onlooker when Mary emerged from the kitchen, said: "Oh Dill!" with her face crumpling, and broke into floods of tears while Dilys hugged her and tried to calm her down. DI Oak's rejected mug of tea finally found a use.

All the story came out. The marriage had been a mistake from the start, Mary could see that now, but it seemed alright the first couple of years. Even though there had been one or two times she suspected Ray of playing away. She had no proof, however, so she stayed. But things hadn't been as happy as they should have. "You know how it is, Dill."

"You'd have to be blind as to not to notice, Mary love."

Then six months ago Mary had bumped into Ray's first wife, Tracey, down at the market. Ray and Tracey's split hadn't been overly hostile because Tracey had rapidly secured herself a rich new bloke. So there hadn't been much need to fight over money. They had also split up a good while before Ray had met Mary, so Tracey held no grudges there. Instead she tended to gloat a little about how well she and her new husband were doing, knowing the Boatswain was an ongoing struggle.

It was very rare that Mary bumped into Tracey - perhaps no more than once a year or so - but this time had been different.

For Tracey sported a huge round belly and was even more smugly pregnant.

Mary offered the usual congratulations and good wishes.

Tracey made a couple of complaints about her feet and fatigue. "But you won't have to worry about that, will you, with Ray?" she said.

Mary wasn't sure what Tracey was talking about at first.

"He's had the chop, hasn't he?"

Ray had never said anything to Mary about it. He knew, in fact, that she wanted kids. To the point of discussing names one time. She'd even started to worry that she'd not already fallen pregnant, though things in the bedroom weren't as regular as they might have been. But she was only in her early thirties so it seemed like there was plenty of time.

Not so, according to Tracey. "You can't mean to say he didn't tell you?" she said to Mary, clearly revelling in Mary's shock. "I didn't want kids, back then anyway, and nor did Ray, so he went to get snipped. He didn't half moan about it afterwards. All he had was a little swelling, gone in a week. Anyway I'd best be off now. Ta-raa."

And Mary's dreams were gone in a matter of seconds. If the rot had set in before, now it deepened and spread. She could barely look at Ray when she got back.

"So who's the father?" Dilys asked.

Mary looked miserable. "You know who it is."

"Not that one, surely?"

"That's the one."

How they knew that they both meant the same person, Perry had no idea. He also had no idea who the person might be. He was feeling very conflicted. He was disturbed to learn about Ray and Mary and the pregnancy thing. He was uncomfortable with knowing such personal details about someone else. He also had a twinge of compunction that Rose had been right and he had dismissed her. *You never believe me.*

Above all, it was none of his business, yet Mary had become a friend. More so than Ray. Thinking of this, and thinking of his own mother, he decided that his sympathies were firmly with her. "If there's anything that needs doing," he muttered, but before anyone could answer he slipped out of the Boatswain and back to his boat.

Perry's mother had been only seventeen when she had fallen pregnant with him. He had been born a week after her eighteenth birthday. Her mother had died a couple of years previously so it was just Emerald and her father. He cast her out in shame.

They never reconciled. Emerald died less than a year later and her father, Perry's grandfather, followed her not long after. Of a broken heart, so Black Bessie had told Perry. It was one of the reasons Black Bessie been able to hang onto him, because no one else claimed him. She wasn't particularly maternal but she could make use of an infant. It was much easier to shoplift pushing a nice roomy pram about.

She also lent him to a friend of hers who claimed child support for him, which they split between them. There weren't so many checks in those days.

Perry didn't remember his early childhood as an unhappy time. He never got hit and there was always food for him, so far as he could recall.

Old Owen had once said something odd to him. "Ah, but we couldn't let you be taken, could we? Not with you being who you were." He had offered no further explanation and Perry had soon forgotten about it. Something awoke the memory years later and though he could have tracked Old Owen down and asked him about it, he never did.

23

Blurred memories. Foggy reminiscences of drunken times.

Yet among it all, Perry thought, someone had said something important. He sensed this quite strongly even though he couldn't recall what it was. He walked back along the towpath, trying to puzzle it out.

Thinking about Mary's unhappy marriage and the divorce job he'd done for Martin, he got to thinking about blackmail. If Mary had a secret from Ray, a huge secret, might someone be twisting her arm over it?

Some of the odd things about her made some sense now. Her going out at night, as Rose had revealed, might well have been to meet that other man.

They were back by the Emerald when Perry returned there. King John and his motley crew. What did they want this time?

"Morning," Perry said. He was out of beers so they'd have to push off to the Stag if they wanted a drink. It would be opening soon, if it wasn't already. As if that was all they'd want, though. Funny time of day for them to show up, too.

"Morning, Beck." King John was looking pleased with himself, Perry thought. Maybe he'd just pulled off a decent job. "Well now, perhaps we'll step aboard?"

"Be my guest."

They crowded onto the small deck again and stood about there. "You'll be wondering why we've come," King John said. He had a crafty look on his face.

Perry did wonder but wasn't going to say it, so King John continued.

"Might have got something for you. Information."

"If it's about Grover, that's all done and dusted. It wasn't exotics either. It turned out to be some beer scam." Perry didn't want King John thinking Perry owed him too much for that one.

"Ah well now, was it or wasn't it?"

King John was in cryptic mood, which Perry didn't have the patience for. "I've got to get the boat up to the yard today," he said.

"Perhaps we'll enjoy a cruise then, lads?"

Perry went to start the motor, praying a silent prayer as he did every time that it wouldn't clap out just yet. Only another couple of weeks. Then they'd be putting the new one in.

King John had gone full pirate by the time the Emerald was moving, regaling the boy Joe with tales of his life "on the main". King John had spent a couple of summers as a boy in Hastings staying with a maiden aunt, many decades ago now, so far as Perry knew.

It turned out that King John had started taking some interest in the whole Grover affair. He'd been following it in the papers and knew that Perry was among the suspects. Plus he had a little bit of insider knowledge from a few sources here and there. He also knew, better than anyone perhaps, that Perry hadn't done it.

"It all boils down to the widow's death, doesn't? Everyone being in the pub when she was shot."

He ought to swap sleuthing notes with Martin, Perry thought.

"It's an interesting coincidence, but the boy Joe here was taking a walk not far from here on the night of the shooting," King John told him.

It turned out that the Company had been over Oxford way on the day of the Midsummer Festival, doing "a bit of business" as King John put it. He didn't specify what this had been, but Perry supposed the Company may have thought it was a good day for doing over a few businesses closed on the weekend. Many of the local police were down at the festival keeping an eye on things there, suggesting less scrutiny on other areas.

Some of the Company had gone drinking until late in the White Stag, the same time at which Perry and his friends were all drinking in the Boatswain. The Stag didn't have a lock-in so everybody was kicked out shortly after eleven. The boy Joe had got separated from the others in the crowd leaving, and sat for a while by himself outside the pub, waiting. No one came since they were too drunk to remember they had left him behind.

So Joe, simple as he was, started walking along the towpath. Except he went the wrong way. This route took him in the direction of Perry's boat and then onto the Boatswain, instead of towards the city.

"And then," King John said with a gleam of triumph, "the boy Joe saw something interesting. Didn't you, Joe?"

"Arr. I seed summat," Joe said. It was the most Perry had ever heard him say.

"Something I dare say the police would be keen to hear, though they won't get it from our lips, isn't that right, Joe?"

"Arr."

"Joe would like to tell you what it was, but information is valuable, isn't it?" King John's cards were on the table.

They had nearly reached the boatyard and Perry got the mooring rope ready. "Depends on what information. Nothing to do with me, the murder investigation."

"You say that now, Beck lad, but there may come a time soon when it's very much your business."

What did King John know, Perry wondered? He waited for the insinuation to be made clearer.

"You consider how they tried to fit Grover up. Planting those bullets in his place. You'd think only the stupidest of scuffers would be taken in by that, but they all fell for it, didn't they?"

King John paused, regarding Perry with a sharp eye. "So whoever it is did this, who do you reckon they'll think to fit up next? If I were you I'd be watching my back and keeping this vessel here well-guarded, Beck lad."

Perry took the bait. "What's this that Joe saw, then?"

The crafty gleam intensified. "We do you a favour, you do us a favour. Just a little matter of a small difficulty Abingdon way. Shouldn't take you more than a couple of minutes at most."

It wasn't an even deal and they both knew it. At this stage Perry had too much to lose by risking taking on a Company job. Even if he'd had the appetite for it which he didn't. He also doubted it would be a one off. Once King John got his clutches into him again that would be it. Endless leverage and pressure.

But if King John's warning was valid, might he one day need the boy Joe's information to clear himself? He hadn't considered that someone might try to frame him.

The more he thought about it, the more likely it seemed. Whoever it was had nearly got away with framing Grover, if only his body hadn't been found. They'd probably hoped to buy a few months' time with that.

It stood to reason they might be on the lookout for another stooge.

Who were they? And what had Joe seen?

Perry wouldn't normally have discussed this type of information with anyone, but Martin was sort of his brief, and a brief was like a priest for keeping things confidential. Because he was worried. He'd seen people get fitted up before and how easy it was. It was a good way of getting rid of troublemakers or at least sending them a good warning.

The thing with Grover though, that took it a step further. He'd possibly been intended as a permanent scapegoat, never to be found nor identified. Stupid, really. Everyone knew that a stiff stank. It was why you avoided it at all costs, King John had always said. Too much trouble than it was worth, disposing of it, in most cases.

So Perry told Martin the gist of what King John had warned. He related it as "advice from an old associate" and Martin didn't probe the source further.

Perry immediately regretted telling him as soon as the words were out, but Martin looked thoughtful.

"I expect it's all a bit farfetched," Perry said. "Best to forget it."

Martin disagreed. "I don't think so. I think we'd all be wise to be cautious, but you know what the cops are like. It's neat for them, past form. Makes the whole thing easier. You ought to keep a close watch over the boat, make sure no bullets get planted on you."

This was easier said than done.

"The thing is with the police, they're a business like any other," Martin said. "They've got a job to do, targets to hit. They're under pressure to get results. They've got three corpses on their hands and they haven't made a single arrest. I don't doubt most of them want to get the real killer. But charging someone - anyone - would be a priority right now. A big win that they need. So even if they guess it's a set up, and that Oak fellow isn't an idiot, he surely would see straight through it, they'll still bring you in for show."

He paused.

"Then the problem is that there'll be another crime somewhere else that takes the focus off the triple killer investigation, and resources are already stretched. They've wound down the hunt because they've got someone banged up and the immediate pressure's off. That's when getting it to stick to you becomes the easiest option."

Perry had a fair idea of all this but hearing someone like Martin saying it confirmed it. It made him more genuinely fearful.

He couldn't stay with the Emerald around the clock because he needed to work. Even if he had been able to, he also couldn't stop someone slipping something on the deck and tipping the police off while he slept.

It was a dilemma. Perry was at a loss.

"The only thing you can really do," Martin said, seeing the worry on Perry's face, "is to find the killer first. Which means doing the police's job for them. But if your skin is at stake, we don't have many options."

Perry was surprised by the "we". "You'd help out?"

"You're our client. It's our job."

It was more than their job though, Perry knew that. Jeff Harcourt would hardly advocate an amateur murder hunt. It was Martin who was keen to solve it, for whatever reasons of his own.

So be it. If Martin's and Perry's goals happened to align, he wasn't going to knock back an offer of help.

But where did they start?

"Something my uncle always says is that you've got to watch for someone acting out of character," Martin told him. "That's always a sign there's serious trouble, he reckons. Not just acting odd, because anyone can act odd. Like a chap starts working late all the time, but actually he's having an affair. Or he's in a bad mood all the time, and it turns out his job is on the line. None of it's really unusual. It's low grade stuff, happens all the time."

Perry thought of Mary. She had been going out at odd times, and getting snappish with Rose. And then it turned out she was seeing someone behind Ray's back.

Martin continued. "The serious stuff is when a client acts out of character against their own nature. It might not even be anything odd for anyone else to do, but it's odd for them."

"How do you mean?" Perry asked. He was intrigued but he couldn't yet grasp the difference.

"Take a couple of examples. We had a client whose husband was a sharp dresser. Designer suits, razor sharp lines, top brands, shiny shoes, the whole hog. Very proud of his appearance. Wouldn't be seen dead with so much as a button missing or a sleeve that was too short. A bit of a joke to his friends. Then one day he goes out and buys a cheap suit. Really cheap and nasty compared to his usual garb. Anyone else might buy a cheap suit for any number of innocuous reasons, but not this guy."

Perry thought it was possible the man had run out of money.

Martin disagreed. "If he had, he'd have more likely stolen a new suit. Or hidden away. Anything to keep up appearances. He was very proud, that was his core nature. And then all of a sudden a cheap, shiny suit appears in his wardrobe. It turned out he planned to bash his wife in the next day and didn't want blood on any of his regular gear."

"He didn't manage it, then?"

"She found out - just in time - that he was screwing his secretary. She moved out to her sister's and called my uncle."

A nasty business, Perry thought.

Martin gave another example. "We had a client who was an art collector. Fancied himself a connoisseur. He claimed to be a great lover of art and that it was painful for him to part with anything. He'd hardly ever sell off a work unless he saw a massive profit on the original price. Maybe the artist had just died, something like that, and it was too good to pass up. Even then he'd groan and lament his sorrows about parting with a work."

Perry knew the type.

"One day he's selling these two paintings - still lifes, of bowls of fruit - and he doesn't seem to care about the sale. Normally he's intensely meticulous over every last detail, but suddenly he's weirdly laid back. My uncle was supposed to be sorting out the contracts of sale and he smelt a rat. It turned out they were forgeries. Uncle Jeff guessed something was up because the man was acting so out of character. Another person might well want to sell off a couple of paintings quickly, just to liquidate some assets, but this client never would have done so. He made such a big deal about adoring every last artwork in his collection, so why the sudden apathy with the still lifes?"

Perry was getting the sense of it but he couldn't yet see how it might be applied to any of the suspects. It would take some thinking about.

Martin had one more piece of advice. "Other than that, never trust anything they say. Any single piece of information, however innocent it sounds, may be a lie. Because whoever did it has been lying through his or her teeth for weeks, and maybe a good while longer."

It took Perry the best part of a year to save up for the narrowboat. Mainly through farm and other labouring work.

While poking around car boot sales for useful tools Perry discovered that items sold for pennies in charity shops might go for a few quid at a sale. He started a sideline dealing in bits of junk. There were already blokes onto collectors' items like old records and comics, and Perry didn't know what to look for there, so he didn't bother with that.

There were TV programmes where people supposedly found priceless old paintings on sale at junk sales, or a vase that turned out to be Ming. Perry never saw that kind of luck.

But children's clothes, bits of costume jewellery: bored women would pick over these at the car boot sale while their men bargained over a broken lawnmower or second hand golf clubs.

It was time intensive work, browsing round the charity shops and hauling his wares to a carpark on Sunday morning. It also meant he had to risk a bit of his capital. But the payoff was more than worth it. He'd easily make ten or twenty quid on a good day. Sometimes more as the season went on and he figured out what people would pay for.

Perry could see how people made a full time living out of this line, but at the end of the day all the wheeling and dealing wasn't really for him. It was simply a means to an end.

24

Perry lay on his bunk in the Emerald. He couldn't sleep. It was a hot night and the stuff Martin and King John had been saying was swirling around in his head. He was physically tired but his mind just wouldn't stop whirring.

He'd given some thought to each of the people who had been at both events: the lock-in and the barbecue. His initial reaction was to rule most of them out. After all, what would Mary be doing running around with guns in her condition? Then he remembered Dilys saying something about hormones and acting crazy, so he kept her on his mental list. He couldn't think of any motives for her. Even if the Boatswain had been scammed by the labelling fraud he couldn't see Mary getting a gun out. Also none of the customers had ever commented on Stanton's Premium tasting on the weak side. So Perry suspected the Boatswain hadn't been on the list of public houses affected.

Damon was an obvious one. He had acted out of character, Perry thought. That odd business about wanting to work down the Brewery when he was normally as lazy as anything. Perry couldn't remember him doing a day's work all summer. Likely he paid Ray and Mary no upkeep either. Plus there were all the drugs he took which wouldn't come cheap. That might be some kind of motive for him. It was hard to imagine him staying sober long enough to aim a gun at someone, but he might have managed it.

He was conflicted about Ray. He'd become aware of Ray's darker side ever since Mary's revelations. No - that wasn't quite accurate - the awareness had started since Rose's allegations, Perry had to admit. At least a part of him had believed the kid. Ray was not such an amiable character as he liked people to think. Even if the Boatswain had escaped the beer fraud, Ray might have had some other business issues with Arthur Stanton. They were in the same industry; there would always be links. Or - Perry remembered Mary's mention of Ray "playing away" - it might be possible he was up to something with Sybil. He couldn't see it himself and she hadn't looked the type, but you never knew.

Next up, Dilys Jones. She had her ear to the ground and could have had her finger in a lot of pies what with her cleaning round taking her to all sorts of places. But wasn't it more likely that someone would do her in, perhaps for hearing or seeing something she shouldn't, to stop her spreading it around? Dilys was very observant and she liked to gossip, but Perry never got the sense that she went actively poking about anywhere. More's the pity, for if she had, she might have stumbled across something useful. Particularly since she had cleaned at the Stantons' house every week.

On to Priscilla. It surely couldn't be her, Perry thought. He wasn't swayed by any lingering affection for the barmaid, but he thought her an unlikely suspect because she didn't really seem smart enough to have shot three people and got away with it. It was the first time

Perry had consciously realised this, that Priscilla wasn't the sharpest tool in the box. It wasn't that she was stupid, she just wasn't as smart as the others. Even Dilys, though she hadn't been to university like some of them, was as sharp as a tack. Then again, could it be an act with Priscilla? Maybe she had seduced old Arthur and Sybil had rumbled them? It still made no sense where Grover came in, though.

The nursery couple next, Frankie and Barney Goodlock. On the surface they weren't much more than a couple of peace loving hippies running an organic nursery. Still, Perry supposed he should consider them individually. First up, Frankie. She was the more intense one of the couple, driven and business minded. Perry sometimes found her a bit hard to take. Always stressing about her plants. Plants died sometimes, didn't they? It was Nature. Funny business to be in, a plant nursery, if you couldn't handle a few things wilting now and then.

Barney was much more laid back. This, combined with his sort of sleepy appearance, gave the impression that he was on the lazy side. But he wasn't at all, as Perry well knew. Barney worked damn hard at the nursery - as did Frankie - putting in long hours, and so far it wasn't paying as well as they hoped. Barney was the expert, of course. He had qualifications in gardening and farming, whereas Frankie had done something useless sounding at university. The name escaped Perry. It was something to do with theatre. "Performance Arts", that was it.

That left Rose, whom Perry didn't even stop to consider, and Martin. He was in some ways the new arrival, the outsider. Could he be playing them all for some sort of game, Perry included?

Hauling the body, now there was another thought. It took some brawn to shift a literal deadweight. Perry wasn't naturally inclined to assume that a man was more likely than a woman to wield a gun or murder someone. If there was anyone to fear in the Company, it was Black Bessie. She was the most ruthless of the lot. Even King John wouldn't dare to cross her.

But when it came to shifting a corpse, not everyone would have been capable of it. Ray and Mary with their respective back problems seemed ruled out, though Perry remembered Martin's warning about people lying. When had Ray's back problem come on? Could it be part of some elaborate alibi? Or might Ray have injured it when he hauled the body to the old well? Either way, it wasn't as though they'd posted medical certificates up at the pub.

Dilys had a fair bit of muscle on her, from the manual labour she did. Perry had seen her haul furniture around when she was cleaning and it was far less effort to her than it had been to Priscilla. Frankie and Barney both dragged sacks and heavy tubs around at the nursery. Damon could supposedly lift a crate or two, or claimed he could, to have got the work at the Brewery.

The other possibility was an accomplice. Mr X. This would make more sense for Sybil's murder. Both doors of the pub had been locked, not that that would have been an issue for Perry. Which was one more thing the coppers could pin on him, that he was the only one there with the means. If only everyone had been a bit more lucid that night. But what with the festival, the spiked brownies, too much sun and far too much booze, it was simply a blur.

Even if the police had started questioning people directly afterwards it might have helped. But it was a good while before they finally tumbled onto the Boatswain link. And one night was much like another, wasn't it? Who could remember what had been said when, or the order in which people went to the bathroom?

Perry tried to be more observant of the others when he next saw them down the Boatswain. He didn't enjoy being suspicious of his friends. Trust had been everything to the Company. As soon as loyalty failed, they were all in danger.

Rose was back down by the canal, bugging Perry about the box. Sybil's supposedly secret box. "You never listen to me but I bet it's all in there. And someone's nicked it, haven't they?"

Perry, winding a bright orange thread to create orange stripes over black, looked up at the girl. Expecting to see sulky defiance, he was surprised to see how intent she looked.

"We need to find her box," Rose persisted.

Trimming off a strip of feather and fixing it to the fly with more orange thread, Perry twirled it in the sun. For a moment he tried to imagine what it might look like to a fish, seeing it from below the water. Dazzled by the wings and colours, missing the thin, deadly curve of the hook.

"It's not what grown-ups do, Rosie," he told her. "In real life they don't go writing down murderers' names and putting them into boxes. What would be the point?"

"To make money."

How would a kid think of that? "How's that, then?" he asked, feigning innocence.

"You threaten them, don't you? You say that you'll give it to the police unless they give you money."

Perry was silent for a while. "Did you hear your stepmother say that?"

"Not exactly." Rose shifted from foot to foot. "But she said to that old Sparks woman that it was very valuable. That someone would pay for it, and that she'd be keeping it safe. I was listening in when they had tea once."

"The first time you came here, when you thought your stepmother was going to do your father in, why did you think that?" Perry asked her.

"I still think that. I reckon she paid someone to do that."

This thought had crossed Perry's mind more than once. Grover might well be the type you'd hire for that. But it still didn't solve who had killed Grover.

"When did you last see it, this box?" he asked.

"Before she was dead, obviously. It was gone after," Rose told him.

"Was it still there the night she died?" Perry finished off the fly and laid it in the small tray next to him on the deck.

Rose had to think about this. "I don't know. I kept meaning to nick it and try to get it open. But she was always around. Then she got killed and I know it was gone then."

She went to pick up one of the flies and Perry quickly called out a warning. "Careful, Rosie, those have got sharp hooks."

It was too late: she had already caught one on her finger. "Ow." She quickly drew it to her mouth, sucking on it.

"They're not toys, they're for fishing," Perry said.

"I know. I just didn't know they had the hooks on them. Dilys had one on a necklace."

That would have been one of the flies Perry had made as a demo to show Frankie, intended for jewellery, without a hook. He'd later given it to Dilys since Frankie had wanted the butterfly style only. "I'll make you one like that. You won't hurt yourself on it."

"I want a real one. Not a pretend one."

They were getting off track. Martin would be better at this, Perry thought. "If you'll be a good girl and come and talk to Martin about what you remember, I'll make you a barbed one. You can choose the colour."

Rose looked mollified. She leant over the bow of the Emerald and ran her hand over the painted letters of the boat's name. "How did you get your boat?" she asked.

"I saved up and I bought her," Perry told her.

"Why's she called Emerald?"

"It was my mother's name."

Rose traced the letters that she could reach. "It's a nice name. For a person and for a boat."

Once the narrowboat was legally his, he named her: Emerald, after his mother. After all the effort in buying her, Perry managed to get a free tow to a new mooring from another boater who was interested in his project. He was going have to learn more about engines and a whole heap of things. Coal-fired, she was, like most narrowboats.

Perry found that staying in one spot, which he did now he lived on the Emerald, helped him find work. He became known as a useful lad, hard working and reliable. A local boatyard hired him for basic work.

The boat folk were a friendly lot. They had a great deal of reverence for the past and didn't like to see old boats lost to neglect. Perry's plans to renovate the Emerald and get her moving again were welcomed by them.

"You're doing God's work there, son."

He got support in small ways. He was doing more and more hours at the boatyard which earned him money and also served as a casual apprenticeship. Sometimes they'd put a bit extra his way, such as leftover paint, or give him a tip off about things going cheap. He was able to salvage and repair a few items that were getting thrown out.

There was still no water or power aboard the Emerald so Perry was relying on a battery lamp and even candles. He matched his waking hours to daylight as there wasn't much he could get done by candlelight. There were showers and facilities at the boatyard so he used those when he needed to. He was hardly used to luxury, so he didn't feel any particular inconvenience.

25

They sat outside the front of the Boatswain on one of the wooden tables, surrounded by tubs of merrily garish scarlet geraniums. It was private enough here, and Perry felt it was more appropriate for Rose to talk to Martin outside, since kids were allowed in the beer garden. He got her a lemonade and a packet of crisps, and the usual beers for him and Martin.

"Rose here reckons her stepmum had this box, with important stuff inside, but it's vanished," Perry said.

"What sort of important stuff?" Martin asked.

Rose shrugged. "I don't know. Could have been letters or something. She was always getting all secretive over it."

"Can you remember exactly when you last saw it?"

The girl thought. "It was there before my dad died. Then it was there right afterwards. Then she showed it to old Sparkly-knickers, and that was after he died. And then I don't remember, then she got shot."

"Sparkly-knickers?"

"Miss Sparks. But I always called her that, because she was so boring."

"Was she a friend of your stepmother?" Martin asked.

"Her only friend. Who else would want to be friends with simpering Sybil?"

Perry wanted to tell Rose not to speak ill of the dead, but when you thought about it, it was a funny thing to require. It wasn't as though the dead could find out and sue you. Nor did the mere act of dying turn a sinner into a saint. And Perry was glad of this. He had always preferred to think of Jake the Flick the way he had always been: wily, irreverent, dodging about here and there. Not as some dull angel sitting on a cloud playing a harp.

So he didn't try to correct Rose. If Sybil had been awful before, and she had certainly looked awful and simpering the times he had seen her, then she doubtless was still. Wherever she was.

"So there's a chance it went missing before she died?" Martin asked Rose.

"I suppose."

"But you can't be certain? Did she ever keep it in different places?"

"It was always under her dressing table," Rose told him. "I never saw it anywhere else."

"Your dad never looked at it?"

"No. Or he'd be alive now, wouldn't he?" The girl's face was bitter, her blue eyes blazed. She was still convinced that Sybil Stanton had arranged for Arthur Stanton's death. Perry could see that she was trying not to cry.

Martin looked at Perry. "We should probably pay a visit to this Sparks woman. I'm sure the police have already questioned her to the last speck of dust, but there may be something else she'll come up with. We'll have to track down her address. You ever been to her house, Rose?"

"No. She always came round ours. She's a silly old woman," Rose told him. "She always calls me 'dearie' and asks me about school."

"You won't need to come with us," Martin told her.

Rose's face fell in disappointment. "But I'm part of your investigation. They always have lady policemen as well as man ones."

Martin laughed. "You can still be part of it. We just won't need you to pay house calls. You stay here and make us a big list of all the reasons someone might have wanted to kill your stepmother.

That would keep her occupied for at least a couple of hours, Perry thought.

Ray came outside. "You alright for drinks?" he asked, noticing the long empty glasses.

"Fine, thanks," Martin said.

"Don't let me hold you up then. There's others would like a table in the sunshine. Drinks are rent for the prime spot."

When he had gone, Martin remarked on Ray's unfriendliness. "Not the most convivial mine host, is he?" He wanted to say "surly bastard" but Rose was there.

"He has his moments," Perry said, not indicating whether these were good or bad moments.

"I told you Mary was nicer," Rose said. She understood far too much.

Perry changed the subject. "Your exam results come through soon, don't they?" he asked Martin. "What will you do afterwards?"

"I'll still have a couple of weeks before I start in London. Assuming I pass, that is. I might take a trip overseas. The South of France, maybe. You should take some time off yourself and come along. An old schoolmate of mine has a villa in Nice. His family are loaded. It's rent-free."

Perry, who had never been abroad, assumed Martin was joking.

"We were going to go to France," Rose said. "But Sybil got sick on boats."

"Not a problem for Perry is it? So what do you reckon?" Martin asked.

"I've got stuff to do here." Holidaying in France wasn't for the likes of him. He didn't even have a passport.

Martin got up to go, not fancying another run-in with Ray. "The offer's open. Assuming neither or both of us are banged up behind bars by then."

Perry could see the attraction of running a nursery. Outdoor work, plenty of space, and it was rewarding seeing the plants grow and flourish. He liked the vegetables best of all because they were useful. It also seemed more of an achievement to end up with a crop of ripe red tomatoes or a dozen large marrows than a few flowers.

He would have liked to have tried growing some himself, but it was one of the disadvantages of living on the water. Unless you had a permanent mooring, you couldn't have a vegetable patch.

Some of the liveaboards did manage to have small gardens on their boats. Perry had seen a few roof gardens and tubs hung over the sides of decks. He had thought about trying it on the Emerald but he had to figure out a few logistical issues first. Passing under bridges could be a problem if you went too high, and leaking tubs led to peeling paint.

Barney and Frankie sold plants to some of the river folk. Barney was thinking of stocking some specialist products for "nomadic permaculture". The problem was capital. This was the downside to the nursery dream: perpetual money issues.

That afternoon Barney was sitting in the small office behind the shop, hunched over a load of papers. He tapped and retapped figures into a calculator, never managing to get the figures he wanted to see.

"It's just not my area, this. We could do with a proper accountant but that's yet another outgoing," he said to Perry who had just entered.

"Things seem to be selling well," Perry said. They'd sold out of most of the new urns and statuary in a few weeks. Barney had also got a waiting list for some of his fruit tree grafts. Regular garden plants also seemed to be going strong.

"But it doesn't balance. We're spending too much on product and the imports still aren't paying off. Frankie keeps insisting it's still early days and interest is picking up but the shipping fees are breaking us."

Perry looked at a couple of bromeliads displayed in decorative urns. "They did alright at the Festival."

"At a huge discount, to a load of half-wasted hippies. We barely broke even. It was more about cutting our losses."

Some customers came in then, a couple of retirement age. They started browsing the seeds and fertilisers and Barney went to help them out. He wasn't a pushy salesman; he simply gave frank and informative advice. The couple bought the products he recommended, and wavered over one of the bromeliads in the urn.

"How might you look after that, then? Would it need full sun?" the man asked.

"They're not frost tolerant. You can have them as a houseplant, one of the smaller ones, or they'll need to go in a greenhouse or conservatory," Barney said.

The man looked disappointed. "Never mind then." He and his wife left with their seeds and organic fertiliser.

"I have to be honest when they ask," Barney said to Perry, reading Perry's mind. "If I tell them to just stick them in a flower bed and water them regularly, it looks bad for us when they eventually die. But not everyone's got a hothouse."

Perry understood. What neither of them said, but both thought, was that Frankie needed to start facing facts.

Barney, who had returned to his accounts, pushed the calculator aside. "Sometimes I think it would be easier just to pack it all in and focus on the crops. There's growing demand for organic veg. A market garden might do alright. We could do more wholesale as well, local restaurants, grocery stores. I could still dabble with the grafts on the side."

But no more tropical exotics. Perry wondered how Frankie would take it. That was the thing when you got tied down with a wife or kids. You couldn't just do your own thing.

The Emerald herself had become a cosy little nook to sleep in. He'd fitted her out with scraps of this and that, much of it scavenged, but he had a comfortable bed, curtains for privacy, and various essentials. He got an old gas stove that was going cheap after being chucked out for a newer system. When he finally got the water tank sorted, this meant hot water, both for washing and for tea.

Perry had mostly been eating basic meals that didn't need heating or refrigeration. Sandwiches, cans of stuff eaten cold. Apples lasted for ages so he bought them from the grocer's or scrumped them when they were in season. Other fresh produce was often beyond his budget or harder to make a meal of. He tried stewing a cabbage once but it went all wrong and he ended up chucking it in the canal.

Life was easy when you had a purpose. Perry never got bored, never complained. Not that he had anyone to complain to. The friends he made tended to be seasonal. They drifted off each winter.

He wasn't a loner by nature but his past had made him wary of trusting anyone. You kept to your own company, whether you liked them or not. Familiar faces were safer faces.

He still had people he could call on. Being a hard worker made him valuable, and if you were valuable, people did more for you.

26

Now that he was actively trying to hunt down their killer, Perry found himself more interested in the victims. Knowing more about them might help him figure out who did it. He knew the police had presumably been all over it, but they might have missed something. He also knew the group of suspects better than they did.

Dilys was the obvious source for inside information on the Stantons. She had volunteered various details over the past weeks but Perry hadn't paid as much attention as he might have.

"What were they like, Arthur and Sybil Stanton?" he asked. He also figured out that if Dilys did have something to hide, he might pick up on it from what she said about her former employers.

"Why d'you ask?"

"Just curious," Perry said. "Wondered why someone might want to do them in."

Dilys had decided earlier in the week to quit smoking, and had chucked her cigarettes away. Arriving at the pub for work she'd had a relapse and managed to get some tobacco and roll-up papers off Damon.

"Thought you were done with those, Dill," Mary said, passing by.

"You know how it is. Just one more. Nightmare of a week."

"Problems?" Mary asked.

"The old Crawshaw witch. Wish someone would do her in. Always fussing and griping." Dilys took a long draft of the roll-up and sighed. "I needed that. So what were you asking, Perry?"

"The Stantons. What were they like?"

"Have you turned sleuth, or something? Are you and Martin planning to beat the boys in blue on the murder hunt?"

Perry wasn't sure why she brought Martin into it.

"He put you up to this, didn't he? He's already asked me every last detail about them. Still, it's no skin off my nose. I've no qualms speaking ill of the dead. Or the living, for that matter."

It struck Perry that Dilys might have done it, even if he couldn't see why. She was also the person most likely to have known about the box Rose was obsessed with. Possibly even to have taken it, given the access she had. "Rose mentioned a box that her stepmother owned."

Dilys was dismissive. "That damn box. Rose was always going on about that. Wanted me to get the thing open for her, as though I've got a skeleton key on my bunch. I told her I was no Perry Beck. That got her asking all about you, of course."

Perry had guessed that Dilys was the likely source of Rose's original interest in him and this confirmed it. "So you never saw inside the box? Sybil Stanton didn't open it up when you were there?"

"Never."

"Any idea what was in it?"

Dilys blew smoke out. "Your guess is as good as mine. Old love letters or photos, most like. These things don't last long, do they?" she said, eyeing the roll up. She still had a pinch of tobacco left so started making another.

"What was she like, then? As a person?"

Dilys thought about it. "On the surface, very prim and prudish. Spinstery, even though she was married. Didn't like kids or animals. Liked things neat. She wasn't very good giving instructions, she'd be bossy and ask for the wrong things. I've seen that with clients that have moved up in life. They're either too embarrassed and humble to ask for anything or they go the other way and turn into a Sergeant Major. Sybil was like that, constantly on your back."

Perry didn't really get what Sybil meant.

"If you live in a big house, there's certain things you do in certain ways, at certain times. Carpet, curtains, linens, silver. If you've come from a small home, you don't know about those things. She didn't have the first clue," Dilys explained.

"You don't reckon she was the type to get into blackmail?"

"Exactly the type. Not the type to make a success of it though. I wouldn't be at all surprised if she botched that up and got a knife in her back. Or a gun, as happened. That doesn't explain Grover, though, does it? Or who killed Arthur, if that's what she was blackmailing someone over."

Who would have wanted or needed all three of them dead? Perry tried to think it through for the thousandth time. Mr X kills Arthur. Either Sybil finds out and blackmails him and he does her in, or he needs her dead as well for whatever reason. Grover finds out, or maybe he was hired to kill one or both of them, then he's threatening to talk so out he goes. Or maybe Grover had to go for the same reason that Arthur and Sybil did.

It all boiled down to the Brewery.

"What about Arthur, any thoughts on him?" Perry asked.

"Never saw much of him. He was at work when I came to clean. He wasn't the best father to Rose, though. And Sybil was even worse. It's why even though I'm sad for her, losing both her parents, I think she'll be better off with that nice auntie of hers up north," Dilys said.

Rose came in at this point with a friend, another girl about her age with her hair in bunches. They were giggling and stuffing sweets into their mouths from two paper bags. Mary came over. "You didn't spend all that money on sweets, did you, Rose?" She turned to Perry and Dilys. "I gave her some pocket money for helping with chores but it was supposed to go in her piggy bank, wasn't it?" She addressed Rose again. "You might need to buy pencils and things for school next term. Your auntie works remember, she might not have time to sort it all out." Rose giggled with her friend and ran upstairs.

"You're getting attached to that kid," Dilys observed.

"I know. She's a nice girl. But there's no way I can give her a permanent place, not with all..." Mary broke off and suddenly looked miserable.

"Have you decided what to do about it yet? Are you going to keep it?"

Once again Perry felt it was a conversation he should excuse himself from. Women's business.

"I can't get rid of it Dill, what if it's my only chance?"

"You'll have to tell him then."

"I can't do that, you know I can't." Mary was despairing.

"It'll come out eventually," Dilys warned.

"I thought I might just go away. Start up again somewhere else."

"He's got a right to know though, hasn't he? And you've got a right to child support."

Mary sat down and Perry used this as an excuse to get up and mumble his goodbyes. As he left he heard Dilys saying: "But if it were different, you'd want to be with him, wouldn't you?" and Mary replying: "I don't know Dill, I just don't know."

At Goodlock Nursery, Perry lingered in the hothouse. A cold wind was blowing that day and summer had decided to hide. So he sat in the warm humidity for a while, taking a break. Most of the worked needed that day was done.

He closed his eyes and tried to imagine what it would be like if the weather was actually like this outside. A country where these absurdly expensive, fragile plants grew like vigorous weeds.

How hot would it be in the south of France? Perry had found himself pondering Martin's offer. Not to take it up, there was a list of reasons as long as the phone book why that wouldn't be possible. But it made him think that he should branch out one day and see a bit more of the world. He had plenty of England to see first though.

Frankie came in. "Enjoying the climate? Not bad on a day like today, is it? Heating costs a fortune in winter of course."

"Reckon you're seeing interest picking up in these?" Perry asked, indicating the tropical plants.

Frankie shrugged. "Business is slow across the board at the moment. Most people have got their gardens set up for the summer. And lots of people take holidays in July and August. Tourists don't really come here, either. But short of some disaster like a flood or a hurricane, we should be okay."

Perry lunched with Barney inside the shop. Frankie had already eaten hers. "If you're going out later, could you stop by the hardware store and pick me up some asphalt emulsion," Barney asked her. "Just a small tub. That sealant I made with the beeswax doesn't look like it's working very well. A few of them have got fungus. I know it's not as eco-friendly but I'd prefer to avoid ending up with a hundred dead trees. That rootstock was five quid a pop."

"I'll see if I can find it."

"Funny thing, gardening," Perry said, after Frankie had gone.

"How do you mean?"

"All those chemicals. You wonder how Nature managed without them."

Barney finished off his sandwich. "Badly. She grows weeds, and lets various pests eat them. But I know what you mean. Even for organic horticulture, we've practically got a lab's worth of powders and potions. It's that or let the slugs feast at our expense."

Chemicals were one thing Perry had to deal with when installing a waste system on the Emerald. How to deal with waste and the different systems involved was an education in itself. The Emerald hadn't had any kind of waste system when Perry found her, so he'd had to invest in putting one in.

He'd heard all the horror stories by then of leaks and spills and odours. He'd even seen a holidaymaker stumble and trip when carrying a toilet cassette to be emptied, and it wasn't a pretty outcome. So Perry didn't cut corners.

He went for a tank system because it was cheaper. At the yard he'd learnt about the plumbing so he knew the best way to put the pipes in. A tank meant he'd have to pay to pump out, but the price wasn't too prohibitive. He still hadn't installed electricity so he was saving on power costs.

It was a strange balance of being independent and self-sufficient but still reliant on some vital services. In the olden days people could just have dumped their waste in the water and there was no electricity to speak of. Now, you could never be entirely disconnected.

Later that day Perry was walking back from the nursery when a car pulled up. It was Martin. Perry could tell from his face that something bad had happened.

"Uncle Jeff just got a call. The police are looking for you. Someone tipped them off that they saw you with a gun. They're all over your boat."

Perry had been expecting this but it was still a blow. "Did they plant the gun there?"

"No, but I think they've found ammo again. The whole thing's absurd. It couldn't be more of a farce if they brought the Keystone Cops in. They must know it's not you, but they might reason that if they bring you in, the actual killer will drop their guard. Maybe slip up."

Perry wasn't so sure. He feared they'd be only too happy to accept him as a suspect.

"Anyway," Martin continued. "I'm supposed to be driving to Goodlock Nursery to bring you back with me, and take you down to Harcourts so Uncle Jeff can accompany you down the station." He looked intently at Perry. "What I thought I might do instead is drive there and find you already gone."

Perry had seconds to decide. It was the slowness of what lay ahead that decided him. Even if he was cleared eventually, it could take weeks or months. And that was if he was cleared. There were no guarantees.

"If it helps you decide, Uncle Jeff says there's zero chance of bail if you're charged with a triple shooting."

"Thanks."

"Just bear in mind, if they didn't plant the gun, they still have the gun."

Not knowing when he might see Martin next, Perry turned and headed towards the river. He jumped in and swam across. When he got to the other side he crouched behind some bushes and could hear, then see, police cars heading in the direction of Goodlock's. He wondered how Jeff Harcourt had got an early tip off. A friend in the force, presumably.

Someone was taking a huge risk for him, and as much as he loathed the police, it gave him the determination not to waste this chance. Dripping wet but barely noticing the cold due to adrenalin, he made his way over the fields, sticking to hedgerows. There should be a stretch of woodland on the other side of the Western By-Pass, once he got to a church.

He knew this, because he had explored the church a couple of years ago. It was where a nun had discovered some magic well. She'd had to hide herself too, in a forest among swine, according to a plaque. It might well be the same stretch of woodland but there weren't so many wild boar there these days.

Crossing the bypass was a job at any time of day, but it was rush hour which made it even worse. Somehow he got across, having to wait on the central reservation to clear the other side. God knew how many drivers of passing vehicles spotted him. There would probably be alerts about him all over the news tonight.

Everything he'd ever been taught came into play now. Somehow Perry felt that Jake was with him, running with him, just behind his shoulder. Crashing through the undergrowth with him.

He had no money on him. Nothing. Just the key to the Emerald. The anger he felt at all the cops tramping all over his boat spurred him on.

The adrenalin got him quite some way into the wood and then he had to stop because he was exhausted. He hadn't yet formed a plan. But he knew there was only one place he could go. One place where he'd be sheltered. And that the price of shelter would not be cheap.

Perry reached the western edge of the wood and waited there until dusk. He drank from a stream. He wasn't overly hungry.

He was starting to think about safe houses. The old woman in the Hampton Pye might be nearest, but Faringdon was still a good fifteen to twenty miles away. On foot he'd get there by dawn but it was a hell of a long time to be out on the road. Better to nick a bicycle and be there in an hour or so.

He came across a bike in the first village he passed. It had a combination lock which was child's play to Perry. A tug and a twist of each dial to get the gaps, and it clicked open. He cycled via the back roads. The bigger danger at this time was being knocked down by another vehicle. The country lane was winding and narrow in places with thick hedges and blind corners.

The day had been overcast and the night was cloudy. There were no stars nor any light from the moon. A good night for Company business, less so for a cyclist riding without a lamp.

Perry couldn't remember what villages he was supposed to pass, only that he was on the right road. It had been years since he'd come this way. They'd driven down on that occasion in a van, following a successful night's thieving in Witney.

On the bike, he'd reach the pub before closing time. It was possible they'd have cops there but he doubted it. The pub had always fallen under the radar, he'd never known of a single raid taking place there. Mind you, he'd been out of the business for years now. It might be a different story these days.

But the fact that the Company still frequented the pub, which he knew from his recent visit, gave him hope. It was situated to the north of the town, near the church with the haunted graveyard. Perry ditched the bike in a large pond about half a mile away. He felt a twinge of conscience as he did this. Chucking away a good bike seemed a waste but he couldn't risk them tracing it. These qualms were eclipsed by his sense of relief as he finally reached his destination.

Inside the Hampden Pye the main room was about half full, about what could be expected for a weeknight. Perry's dishevelled state drew a few eyes, but it was an establishment where people kept themselves to themselves. Attention was soon returned to beers.

The beady-eyed old landlady was at the bar. "What can I get you?" she asked Perry, looking him up and down. His clothes had more or less dried over the past hours but he knew he must look a state. He reached up to his hair and found a twig there, which he brushed off.

He lowered his voice, coming straight to the point. "I need to get word to King John."

Her eyes narrowed. "In a spot of bother are you?"

"Something like that."

"Should we be awaiting callers?" The old woman's eyes flicked to the door and back, as if expecting police officers to burst in any moment.

"Hopefully not." Not yet, anyway.

"You'd best come round the back."

Perry was admitted to a small private room in the back of the pub. He had very faint memories of it. Someone else had been on the run years ago and King John had gone there to sort things out. The Company provided cover where they could.

The room had an old wooden table, heavy and dark with age, and a couple of wooden chairs. A dark green curtain hung over the only window, its fabric thick and light-blocking. A worn wingback chair was positioned by an empty fireplace. Perry had a memory of King John sitting there, warming his hands by a fire. It must have been winter when he had been here before. Summer would at least make it easier for him to live rough if King John couldn't help him.

"I'll see someone sends word," the old woman said. "Looks like you could do with an ale."

Perry indicated his pockets, empty of money or a wallet. "Came in a bit of a hurry," he said.

"Ah well, that's to be expected. No need to worry, all part of the service. Can't have a Kingsman go thirsty." She returned with a pint mug and he thanked her.

Perry sat by the fireplace, drank the ale, and waited. He was bone tired. As fit as he was, his limbs ached for sleep.

But he knew he was safe. That was the thing about sanctuary: once offered, it was absolute. It was too deep a violation of all codes and expectations for the landlady to call the cops on him now. There was no point wasting worry on anything else at present. At a time like this you could only take things moment by moment.

Perry had never become entirely cut off from the Company. There was still a link there, an invisible umbilical cord. They still regarded him as one of theirs and always would. They remained the only family he had ever really had.

From time to time he'd encounter one or other of them. Generally only those on the periphery. They were cordial enough but there was always a wariness there.

He even got approached for jobs. "Easy little gig out Iffley way. We'd make it worth your while, how it about it?" But he always turned them down.

King John never came though, nor did Perry receive any direct messages from him. He wondered from time to time if a couple of the people he bumped into had been instructed to look out for him. Perry knew his skill remained valuable.

The ability never left him. He'd picked up a couple of old locks in junk shops, often interested in one that looked unusual or different. Few of them challenged him, and then only because they were rusty or damaged. He challenged himself with different handicaps such as rubbing a lock one-handed. With certain locks it was easy to master.

Sometimes he fantasised about lock design. How one might make a trick lock that resisted the usual methods. Even as he dreamt these up, he also dreamt up the method to solve them. There were unpickable locks out there, Perry had no doubt, but they were few and far between.

28

"Always there to help out one of the family."

King John obviously considered Perry was back in the fold and for now, Perry didn't have much choice about it.

He must have drifted off to sleep because he was awoken by their arrival. He was relieved and grateful to see King John and the ever-present ghost of Old Owen lingering behind him.

"Got yourself in a fix then, Beck lad?"

"Not by my own efforts."

"We'll have explanations later," King John told him. "Best we get to a safer place for now."

Perry had no idea what the time was but as he stepped back into the pub with them, he saw that it was long past closing time. The place was empty. There was no one but the beady old landlady, who let them out and bade them farewell.

"Farewell to you also, and never fear that your continued help won't see our gratitude," King John told her.

A battered Ford Escort was parked outside. Old Owen was driving, King John sat in the front, and Perry was in the back. It was like the old days. King John was in a jocular mood, doubtless due to having leverage over Perry once again. "It's good to be back with the old Company, isn't it?" he said.

Old Owen took the wheel and drove them towards Swindon, then turned off just as they reached the outskirts of the city. The road now took them past an industrial estate. "Roman road this," he said.

Some way along the road they turned off and headed down country lanes, ending up at what in the darkness appeared to be an old farm. Old Owen drove the car into a large shed. They got out, he closed the doors, and led Perry through a door in the back. It was part of an annexe to the farm: outbuildings or perhaps an old cottage later converted into a more modern dwelling. It had the feel of the Company about it.

Folding chairs and tables in the main room and cheap iron bunkbeds in the upstairs room suggested it had once been used as a holiday let. There were mattresses and blankets, which Perry was grateful to see.

"We could all do with a snooze," King John said. "But first we'll sit up and discuss the suds you're in."

He and Perry took seats around the table, Old Owen hovering behind.

"You go and rest your bones, Uncle," King John said. "The lad and I have got some catching up to do."

Old Owen loped off upstairs.

"So then," King John began. "Let's have it. Though I've a fair idea of what the trouble may be.

Perry explained about being fitted up for the triple killer murders. "I saw it coming. I should have scarpered earlier," he said.

"Always the benefit of hindsight. Still, what's done is done. Scarpering might have brought them down on your back faster. So what's the plan?"

This was where Perry felt at something of a loss. The plan had been to sniff out the killer before the police did. He was hardly free to go around investigating now, and he doubted Martin's chances of cracking it. Martin hadn't known most of them for as long or as well as Perry had. He was still an outsider.

King John clasped his hands over his knee. Then he leant forward. "It may interest you to know, Beck lad, that your needs are once again aligned with ours. For I've kept an ear to the ground about these shootings. You need us, and we require a little bit of your charm for our purposes. Those purposes may be one and the same. It's a single job I'm talking about."

Perry was curious. He had expected King John to rope him into a few pieces of work in return for cover. To find that King John had an interest in the triple killings was unexpected. He said so.

King John sat back again. "Now you'll remember me telling you about a nice little trading operation we've got going Swindon way. Good little local business, nothing ambitious. We leave that to others. Only others is not happy. Others is accusing Company members of encroaching. I know my members, Beck, and they stick to their own patch. It's always been the way and it's the way now."

He gave Perry some more detail. The exotics trade the Company had taken over in the Swindon area was prospering. But there was a flood of the stuff reaching towns to the north and east, and the gangs running those areas were getting vexed, as King John put it. They were starting to harass Company members on the fringe of

Company territory. This harassment took the form of threats, beatings and escalating violence.

"We don't operate past Banbury and they should know that. And that's our other businesses we do there. The exotics don't go past Swindon. We've not touched Oxford. Milton - Northants - even Leicester, you'll see it's all to the north east. It's not coming from Birmingham way. So they reckon it's coming from Bristol via Swindon, and that puts us in the frame."

King John was keen to get to the bottom of things. When he'd heard about Grover and guns, he'd suspected some serious business and started digging. "We've had a tip off about that brewery. There's something queer going on down that way." He put up a hand to silence Perry. "I know all about your little investigation there. Word gets out. But it needs checking out again."

"It was only a bottling scam," Perry told him. "A switch of the labels. Grover may have been involved in the printing, that was the only link I could find. It was all over months ago."

"That's as may be. But when one business folds, another opens. It's that new business that concerns us."

The plan was to get up to Oxford and take a proper look around the brewery. Perry sensed King John still knew more than he was letting on but that was his way. He never disclosed all his information. This was where Perry came in. His lock picking skills and his inside knowledge of the place made him ideal for the job.

"It'll just be the three of us. You to get us in, Uncle to drive and stand watch, and me to find what we're looking for."

It was a serious job indeed if King John himself was taking such a central role.

"We won't be taking anything?" Perry asked.

"Most probably not, no. Seems a shame, don't it, all that free ale? This one's on the riskier side and we don't need slowing down."

"And then what?"

"If we find what I suspect we may find, then we'll have got a little more to work with, won't we?" King John, master of the cryptic, said. "For now it's time for a good snooze. And a day of some leisure tomorrow, at our little country estate here."

With King John snoring and Old Owen wheezing in his sleep, it took Perry a while to fall into slumber himself. He was shattered on every level and had gone past the stage of easy sleep. Instead he lay awake for hours, exhausted. He missed the sounds of the river and the feeling of sleeping on water. The Emerald was a steady boat and barely rocked on the canal unless another craft came past.

But here, on the top bunk in this upstairs room, Perry felt high, dry and stranded.

He wanted relief and peace of mind, to know where he was, but that was something you could never get with King John. King John always had his own agenda that he wouldn't disclose, buried behind all the other plots and plans.

Perry also had a gnawing hunger. The last meal he'd eaten had been a sandwich at Goodlock Nursery, and he'd expended a huge amount of energy since then.

Knowing from long experience that King John never let Company members go hungry, for a grumbling belly was a distraction, Perry slipped off the bunk and went down the stairs. The fridge was off and there was nothing in it. He tried a cupboard. The first one had plates and cups. He tried another and found a few cans. Potted meat, baked beans, sardines. A tub of mustard powder and a damp looking box of bicarbonate of soda. It wasn't much of a midnight feast.

He opened the sardines with the key on the back of the can - a funny thing to call it a key, for it wasn't at all - and found a fork in a drawer. He sat down at the Formica table and tucked in. The tin of fish got him thinking about the perch he had planned to catch and cook. If he ever got out of this current fix, he resolved, he would make that a priority.

To his surprise, Old Owen drifted into the room. He moved so quietly that he didn't even startle Perry. "Feeling peckish?" he asked. He took a seat at the table.

"There's some beans in there," Perry said, thinking that Old Owen might be hungry. But the other man declined.

"It's rare I sleep through these days. These early hours are a quiet time for thinking."

What on earth did Old Owen think about? Perry had never imagined him as a philosopher.

"Seems to me you'll be doing some thinking yourself," Old Owen said. "Big choices ahead."

Perry looked at Old Owen to read his meaning but his face gave nothing away. "How do you mean?" Perry had to ask.

"Done well for yourself, haven't you? Might be a shame to throw all that in. The old ways are dying off. You've seen we're forced to take on trades we wouldn't have touched a few years ago." Old Owen tapped his forefingers lightly on the edge of the table. It was a habit that Perry remembered from long ago. "I'll say no more. You get back to bed, and a good rest to you."

The luxury of sleeping by himself, in his own space, had always remained a valued prize to Perry. It came from his earliest days when even with the Company there wasn't much privacy and you could get moved on at a moment's notice.

His whole life seemed to have been spent in communal arrangements. Shared bedrooms in foster homes, the children's home, the detention centre. Barns, sheds, campsites.

Once the Emerald was all his, it was at the back of his mind that he could always offer lodgings if times got tight. There were always people prepared to hand over a couple of quid for a safe, dry spot to sleep. He'd been one of them once.

Sitting in the cabin he had no one and nothing to disturb him. He was the captain, the lord of his floating domain. As soon as she was ready to travel, the whole river would be his.

He had a map of the waterways. To Perry it was a map of a thousand adventures and unknown treasures. He could reach anywhere: London, Wales, the Humber, the Irish Sea.

He wondered what Jake would have made of it all. Whether he'd have quit the Company and come travelling as well.

29

It was a day of doing nothing, just waiting around. Perry remembered many such days from his childhood with the Company. The endless wait for nightfall when business could begin.

He felt the same increasing adrenalin as he had done all those years before. At least once he became aware of what he was doing. Now, though, it was an even sicker feeling. Not a feeling of excitement but more one of dread, and regret. He'd known back then, as a boy, that he was making bad choices. Or being made to make them.

But then this Brewery gig wasn't a job in the traditional sense. They weren't robbing. King John solely wanted information, or so he said. Having already looked around the place himself, Perry wasn't really sure what they might find there. It would be child's play for him at least. He already knew the locks, the alarms, the layout.

It struck him that the police might also be keeping an eye on the place so they'd have to be careful.

Lunch was a sausage roll and a can of drink that Old Owen brought back from a service station. The Company didn't keep vehicles for long, at least not after a major job, and Perry suspected tonight would be the Ford

Escort's last trip. It would be passed off to someone else, swapped for some other battered old conveyance, or simply abandoned.

They held a summit while they ate. King John picked Perry's brains about the Brewery. What alarm systems there where. The layout. What was locked and wasn't. Whether there was a night watchman, which fortunately for their purposes, there wasn't.

"All looks good to go then," King John said. "I won't jinx it by calling it a breeze. But a softer job I've rarely seen."

Perry slept in the afternoon as there was nothing else to do and they'd be up all night. There wasn't even a television, though if Perry had seen himself on the news he might have got rattled. Part of him was planning for the worst and what he'd do if it did happen, and he got locked up for a while. He'd have to find some sort of caretaker for the Emerald. He couldn't think who. Boat life wasn't for everyone, though it was a way of avoiding rent. Perhaps there were agencies you could rent it through. Martin or his uncle should know. The lack of electricity might be an issue there.

Old Owen produced a pack of cards and he and Perry played while evening drew on. Old Owen's long fingers shuffled and dealt the cards in a range of intricate ways. He had all the tricks. Riffling, cutting, spreading, fanning them in an arc and flipping them over. Perry remembered how fascinated he had been as a boy when first seeing this.

"How did you learn all that, then?" Perry asked. He had never thought to ask before.

"Uncle of mine ran a gaming club, many years ago now. Used to scuttle around there as a boy. All underground of course, long before they made casinos legit in the sixties. We had some fancy folk there, mind. One woman all in furs who afterwards they said was a duchess. Not that I'd know either way. But a few fancy dealing tricks, it was all part of the show."

Old Owen was much more voluble away from King John, Perry considered. King John had gone out somewhere and they were awaiting his return.

"Didn't want to continue in the business yourself?"

"Never an option," Old Owen said. "It got shut down, and then there was the war. Everything changed after the war."

Looking at Old Owen you might have thought he meant the Great War. Perry found it hard to imagine him as a boy though he supposed he must have been one once.

Perry remembered they still hadn't told him what the boy Joe had seen. Maybe King John would tell him after this job, if it came off. "The boy Joe, where's he from?" he asked Old Owen.

"Some cousin of Bessie's, he's her kid. The Company took him on for a favour, but I can't see as it's working out," Old Owen said.

Perry nodded. Before he could reply the door opened and King John entered.

"Well now, are we supped and ready? It's a fine night for it," he said. There was the familiar gleam in his eye. He had never lost his taste for adventure.

It was a thin crowd to be heading off with, just the three of them. Once more Perry sat in the back of the car as Old Owen drove towards Oxford. He went by the main road and Perry sat low in the car, watchful for any police vehicles. King John noticed this.

"Never fear, they won't have their eye on this motor," King John said. "Bought fair and square from a very respectable cove out Redding way. Can't be too careful with a set of wheels these days."

They left the car in a side street about half a mile from the Brewery and went the rest of the way on foot. If the police came they'd split three ways so at least one or two of them got away. If this happened it would always be King John who escaped, though how he did it, Perry never knew.

Perry kept to the shadows as he walked, avoiding the sickly glare of street lights. It brought his mind back to the photos retrieval job he'd done for Harcourts. Back in the day it was second nature to slip along by the darkest routes.

They reached the Brewery. There were no police cars that Perry could see, but any fears he had were gone regardless. He always got like this, once he was focused on a job. A strange and steady sense of calm overtook him, and he simply did his duty as quickly and cleanly as possible.

He had fashioned what he needed earlier in the day, so the doors opened to them as though Perry had simply unlocked them with a key. No one spoke but Perry could feel King John's eyes on him and felt he could read his thoughts.

Perry disabled the alarm. He knew the codes from when he worked there. While he hadn't ended up needing them, he'd kept an ear out just in case. He had thought he might need to do some night snooping for the Harcourts job but as it turned out, it hadn't been required.

Using torches that King John had supplied, they hunted around. Perry wished he had a better idea of what he was looking for. King John wanted to see inside some of the lorries parked outside, ready for the morning pick up. So Perry got him in and held watch outside until King John was done.

"Nothing there," were his only words to Perry as he exited.

It was frustrating. Normally with a job you got inside and you knew what you were looking for. Often a safe. You located it, the cracker did his business, you got the goods and you made a quick exit. This job was vague.

King John wanted to look through the huge stacks of crates ready for the dawn loading. The first loads were readied the evening before and lined up according to their respective consignments. They'd still be double checked before loading. Particularly since the labelling scam, Fred had told him. But they were essentially in order.

"We'll try the Milton ones. Which lot are they?" King John asked.

Perry hauled a few down for King John who looked over them, turning a couple of bottles, frowning. They all wore thin gloves when on Company business. Old Owen had thrown Perry a pair back at the cottage. Perry preferred to pick a lock with bare hands but he could manage it either way. As a boy he'd even practised with thick woollen mittens as part of his training.

It was perhaps only because Perry had spent years developing a sensitivity to weights and balances that he noticed something odd with one crate he lifted. He was so attuned to noticing discrepancies that it made him pause for a moment as he lifted it back up. King John had already looked it over and discounted it.

It should have had a different centre of gravity. It should have weighed on his left arm more than it did.

He brought it down again.

"Something up?" King John asked.

Perry wasn't sure. He rocked the crate. It was heavy but it wasn't even. He set it on a lower stack and pulled out a bottle from the lighter side. As he drew it out it appeared normal but its bottom was a different story. It had been cleanly sliced open and the bottle was stuffed with something.

Perry pulled the contents out. Small plastic packets containing a white substance scattered on the ground before him, he held one between his fingers.

"Aha," King John said, more than satisfied. "How much is there?"

They checked out how many of the false bottles were in that particular crate, and found more of them in a couple of other crates.

"That's been cut, for that volume. Wouldn't you say, Uncle? Uncle has become quite the chemist since we started up our Swindon subsidiary. Got to ensure production quality, haven't we? No need to sample this lot. But we know where we are now. We'll take a bottle for evidence, as the scuffers would say, and make a tidy exit."

Perry was able to re-alarm and re-lock some of the doors on the way out. With luck the Company's little escapade would pass unnoticed.

He felt that old surge of adrenalin return. The feeling of accomplishment. They'd succeeded, and so far had got away with it. Funny how a job that wasn't even about money or loot had ended up feeling just as big as a win.

Some of the lads he'd laboured with on farms and elsewhere had gone on the dole when a job ended. Perry never did. The Company had avoided all that: benefit fraud was small beer compared to their other sources of income. And the last thing they wanted was for officials to be keeping closer tabs on them.

If anyone was doing it tough, King John put a bit of cash their way. Otherwise they might take unnecessary risks out of desperation or worse, turn informer. "Extra wages" he called it, though regular wages weren't paid in the usual way. It was a flat fee per job, often with a split of takings, at a rate decided by King John.

He encouraged enterprise: if Company members wanted to dabble in their own small gigs on the side that was up to them. Jake had always continued to pick a few pockets down the market or among the crowds of Saturday shoppers in town. It was more of a habit for him than anything.

But the big money was with the Company's official jobs. Just one big hit might have earned Perry enough to buy the Emerald outright when he first found her, or fix up all the things she needed. The thought of it still hadn't been enough to tempt him back.

Labour was labour, whoever you worked for. But the Emerald was bought with honest labour. He didn't owe anyone for her. She couldn't be confiscated.

30

King John liked to hold a debriefing after a job. He considered it a business-like way of affairs. Normally this might take place in a pub with a good meal and an air of celebration, once the merchandise had been carefully stowed. But with Perry's delicate situation, it was safest to return to the cottage. Even picking up food this late at night was a risk.

Back seated around the table, drinking brandy from a bottle that King John had unearthed, they went over the night's work.

"We've solved half the puzzle then," King John said. "It's coming out of Oxford alright, transported to the north on the brewery routes. Nothing to do with our little operation in Swindon. We can tell our friends where they need to be looking, and if they might be so obliged as to stop bashing our boys up."

He was very satisfied. He had been vindicated in his suspicions and the job had come off without a hitch.

"Of course this doesn't yet fix your dilemma, Beck lad," King John said. "Might even make it worse. Your little job down the brewery puts you even more in the spot now. But it's worth betting that this is the reason the

Stanton man was done in. Likely he tumbled to it, and that sort of volume is high stakes. Whoever's running that wouldn't want interference."

He put his cup down on the table. In the absence of liquor glasses they were drinking the brandy out of tea cups.

"We can put the pieces of that gig together anyway," King John said, speaking Perry's own thought processes out loud. "Someone's getting the stuff in, already cut or they're cutting it, getting it to the Brewery and getting it out on the lorries. They'd need someone inside to manage the loaded bottles. That would be Grover. I knew as soon as I heard George Grover's name connected with that place that he'd have been up to some trick or other. If it wasn't filching beer it would be some other game. Then one day Arthur catches Grover at it, or suspects and threatens him."

"You reckon Grover did him in?" Perry asked.

"Could be, could be. Might have been the mysterious Someone. There's no way a cove like George Grover would have masterminded a scheme like this. He would have been on someone else's pay. He or his boss did Stanton in, then they did the wife in, perhaps she knew or they feared she did? Then Someone does Grover in. Probably became a loose cannon, knowing Grover. Never did have much nerve."

Perry remembered the shabby, furtive looking creature he'd met at the nursery and couldn't disagree with this.

"Your task, then, is to figure out which one of your mates down the Boatswain is packaging up these pretty little crystals." King John waved the packet of powder at Perry."

Perry was already going through everyone in his mind. Ray seemed like an obvious choice because of his links with the Brewery, being a customer. He could have easily hollowed out bottles and hidden them with the rest of the empties. You wouldn't notice the weight discrepancy nearly so much with empties.

His nastiness towards Mary, might that all be due to stress at everything starting to unravel?

Another thing with Ray - and also Mary - was that they could have slipped out the back on the night of the lock-in. Perry couldn't remember whether they had both been there all the time. If they had been in league with one another it would have been easier. Given the marital problems, this seemed less likely. Unless Ray was holding Mary's arm behind her back, coercing her into it all.

Everything pointed to Ray: he was at the centre of the web. When the cellar got cleared out for the new dispensing system, that might easily have been to cover his tracks, lay low for a while. If Mary wasn't involved she likely suspected something. Perry started to fear for her safety, and for Damon's. If Grover had been done in then the two of them might well be next on Ray's hit list.

And yet it didn't fit. It did fit, but it wasn't as satisfying as it should have been. Perry found that he wanted it to be Ray. Of all of them he liked Ray least.

It was all going round in his head. He needed to sleep on it. He also wondered what role - if any - the Company would play now. If they got the name of the person behind it, they'd pass that on to the other lot who would likely mete out their own justice. Torch the pub, perhaps. Perry thought of little Rose sleeping upstairs, and Mary with her unborn kid, and felt sick. He'd have to warn them somehow.

But he was getting away with himself. He still needed to know, deep in his bones, that he was right and that it was Ray. He also couldn't just do as he pleased with the cops on his back. It was all overwhelming. Time to get some snooze.

He might have expected to have strange, twisted dreams after such a night, but instead Perry slept like a log. No inspiration came in the night. He didn't sit up in his bed in the early hours with a sudden revelation. Instead he woke feeling groggy and unrefreshed.

It was also late in the morning. King John and Old Owen were long up, and there was a good spread laid out on the table in the downstairs room. One of them had fetched a loaf of sliced bread, some ham, cheese and marmalade. Compared to the past couple of days it was a feast.

Old Owen was chewing a piece of well buttered bread. King John had just taken a swig of tea from a mug and exhaled the steam with a sigh.

Perry gave them a nod. He took a plate and sat down, looking over the food and deciding what to start with.

"Would've got some bacon, but there's no facilities to cook it," Old Owen said. "Gas is out. Electric kettle works, though."

Perry took some ham, rolling it up to eat it with his fingers. "What was it Joe saw?" he asked King John directly. He saw no reason for it to be held from him any longer.

King John paused. "Well now, I suppose as you've a right to know as anyone. It may help you, it may not."

"Go on, then."

Not used to being harried, King John's eyes narrowed. He liked to take his time. Perry knew this but he didn't want King John thinking that he was back under his sway. This was one job, and it was done, and he figured his debt was paid. One job for a couple of nights of sanctuary, and then they could all be on their way again.

"You'll remember it was the solstice, the night that woman was done in." King John liked to keep to the old calendars. "You'll also recall that the boy Joe took a wrong turn. He's a good boy, but he's slow." Perry flicked his eyes to Old Owen at this but Old Owen continued munching his bread. "He walks on for some way, it's a mile or so between the two establishments, and as he approaches the second one, he spies something."

King John paused again and Perry knew this was for effect. He kept his face deliberately impassive.

"He sees the pub - the Boatswain - and then he sees someone climb out of a window on the ground floor, and head towards the towpath. The boy Joe's rattled by now and the figure's some way away. Whatever his reasons he turns tail and heads back towards the Stag. And that's it, that's what he saw." King John looked satisfied and awaited Perry's reaction.

"Was it a man or a woman?" Perry asked.

"Ah, well, now as I've mentioned it was dark and some distance away. All he could say was that it was a figure."

"An adult or a kid?"

"From the way he described it, an adult. Or a very tall kid. He's slow, Joe, as I've said, but he would have remarked on it being a little'un," King John told him.

Perry's mind was turning on two things. First, that this was more confirmation that one of the pub crowd was involved. There was a window at the end of the small corridor between the gents' and ladies' lavatories. Likely it was that one, he thought. The other window on that side looked into the main bar so it could hardly have been the one used.

His second thought was that Ray and Mary would hardly need to climb out of a window. Creeping out the back door would have been less hassle, quicker and also easier to explain if someone spotted them. They lived there, it was their door and their back garden.

Did this mean, then, that Ray was now ruled out? Perry felt a pang of regret because out of all of them, it would have been easiest if it had been the publican.

He found it hard to suspect those around him. They'd become friends, after all. Some more so than others.

But then there was Rose. Somehow he felt he owed her. She had come to him for help and he had turned her away, dismissed her concerns. Even though it might have made no difference if he had taken her seriously, maybe he should have done something.

And if he got evidence that one of them had done it, he'd have little choice but to tip the police off, as much as it went against his nature to do so. But for the sake of his own skin, it would be necessary.

Fitting someone up transgressed all codes of honour. You no longer owed the informer silence.

Trust was everything with the Company, among themselves. You couldn't afford to be betrayed.

It was a precept that Perry carried with him long afterwards. Once he trusted someone he was absolutely loyal to them. It was one reason he was such a reliable worker, because it was against his ethic to let a friend down.

One for all and all for one. Like Musketeers, Jake had said.

"They swore blood oaths in the old days," he told Perry. Jake took his knife out and ran the flat of his blade over his forearm. "Here. They'd cut and mingle the blood. Some groups still do. It leaves scars."

Perry wondered who. "Have you seen them? The scars?"

Jake looked cagey. "Maybe once."

Perry wasn't sure if he was lying or trying to hide something. There were still things he suspected they kept from him.

But the Company's code was clear. If someone was apprehended by the police, they stayed silent. No matter what sort of deal they were offered. When the raid had gone wrong and Perry was in the dock, he didn't breathe a word about the others and he was confident they didn't breathe a word about him.

It was a bond they had, a link that even now he shared with King John and Old Owen. Old loyalties that were thicker than blood, despite all the years apart.

31

Perry resolved to head back to Oxford the next day, though King John wouldn't hear of it at first.

"You're safe now, Beck lad, what would you want to be doing throwing yourself to the wolves?"

But Perry couldn't spend the rest of his life in hiding. Now he knew about the drugs, and the field was starting to narrow, he needed to get back and finish it all.

"If you're set on it, then, Uncle will drive you back. No point getting picked up by the scuffers before you even get there," King John offered.

Perry hadn't yet figured out where to go as Old Owen starting driving towards Oxford. The Emerald and the Boatswain would be crawling with police. They'd likely be watching Goodlock Nursery too, and Harcourts.

He needed to get a message to Martin. The question was how?

"I've got to get in touch with my brief," he told Old Owen.

"He'll want you to turn yourself in," Old Owen said.

"Maybe." Jeff Harcourt would, no doubt about that, but Martin might be up for a game of chance.

They were driving past fields now, that looked arid under the sun. There had been little rain that summer and many long, hot dry spells. "Been doing it tough, the farmers," Old Owen said as they passed desiccated looking cornfields. "Not as bad as the summer of seventy-six of course. Hottest on record, that was."

Perry thought of the plants at the nursery and the irrigation system. He wondered if Barney had managed to get it working again.

"They'd be smarter to put in some dry weather crops," Old Owen continued. "My mother's side was a farming family, and they'd switch to barley and millet in hotter years."

"How would they know?" Perry asked.

"The old ways. They had charts and all sorts of almanacs. That's what country people used, before all these TV weathermen," Old Owen said. "Sustainable. That's what they call it these days."

Old Owen was a wealth of information, Perry thought, as they reached the outskirts of Oxford. Then he had a feeling which some might describe as one's blood running cold.

Except Perry couldn't feel his blood at all. Instead, the fog muzzling his mind, the jumble and confusion that had fuzzed up his head for weeks, was suddenly dissipating. It was more like blocks were falling into place. He marvelled at how quickly his brain started ordering everything after the first two puzzle pieces fitted together.

"I think you've solved it, Uncle," he said.

Like the flash-flash-flash of a camera bulb, memories were re-emerging. Scenes from the barbecue. Snatches of conversation. Remarks that had seemed meaningless at the time.

"Solved what? World peace?" Old Owen wheezed with laughter.

"The triple killing. Something you said." Perry knew now. He knew it in his bones, in a way that he hadn't when it had all seemed to point to Ray.

He remembered what Martin had said, about people's true natures. What it indicated when they seemed to behave against them. Had Martin also realised? But no, Martin didn't know everyone as well as Perry did. He wasn't there so often. He hadn't worked alongside these people.

Proof though, that was a different matter. Most likely any evidence would have been long cleaned up.

Rose Stanton came into his mind then. The box. Maybe if they could get this legendary box, they'd find something there. But where was it? Either Sybil had hidden it, or it had been stolen and possibly destroyed.

As Perry thought all these things, and how the net was finally closing in, he saw where the danger lay.

"I need you to do me two favours, Uncle." Old Owen was under no obligation to help, but Perry sensed that he would.

"Ask, then."

Briefly Perry told him what he needed. He hoped that it wouldn't be too late.

Wearing a university branded sweatshirt and baseball cap acquired by Uncle Owen, most probably nicked but that didn't matter, Perry sat on a bench in the city centre. He looked indistinguishable from the myriad of tourists that thronged Oxford in summer.

He waited there for Martin, who he trusted would come. He'd only sent the briefest of messages to Martin via Old Owen. To fix up an interview with the Sparks woman, and to meet Perry in town.

After a quarter of an hour or so, Martin came and sat on the same bench. It was lunchtime and he had a bag of sandwiches. He ate them, looking ahead of him but talking to Perry as he did so. "I got the address. Thirty-seven Hill Street, past Osney Bridge, off the Botley Road. I'll give it half an hour before I leave."

As if ignoring him, Perry rose and wandered off. It wasn't more than a mile or so. He could have taken short cuts through smaller streets but instead he stuck to the main thoroughfares, blending with the crowds.

Hill Street ended in a cul-de-sac with a recreation ground just past it. Perry sat on another bench and waited again.

Sure enough, after half an hour Martin showed up. He handed Perry a bag. "Put those on."

They contained a cheap pair of tinted glasses with wire frames. Perry lifted them up. They were regular glass, without any magnification.

"It's your eyes, they're noticeable. If anyone's seen you on the news they'll recognise you. And some will have done, make no mistake about that."

Perry put them on, and the world took on a warm beige hue.

"And then this." Martin had a small backpack from which he unrolled a suit jacket. "We'll say you're some sort of clerk. No, we'll just tell her what's the truth anyway. That you're a private inquiry agent we've hired to work on the case. After all she ought to be glad. It's her friend's murder we're trying to sort out."

"What's your uncle's take on all this?"

"Didn't tell him a thing. He wouldn't want to know. When that grey ghost of a fellow showed up asking for me, he left me to it and went off to see a client. Not that I had much to tell him as your bloke wasn't exactly forthcoming. I'm still in the dark. You'd better fill me in."

Perry gave him an account of the Brewery visit and what they had found.

"Drugs. That makes some sense, I suppose. Much higher stakes and more money than that bottling thing you found. So who's behind it?"

Until he had evidence, Perry was reluctant to tell even Martin. Also because it was so obvious he was starting to wonder whether he was wrong. It was too obvious. The fact that they hadn't all guessed ages ago was bizarre.

"I've got no proof yet."

"But you've got a good idea?" Martin asked.

"A notion of sorts."

Martin looked intrigued but didn't press further. "So long as it's not actually this Sparks woman. I didn't come armed."

"No, not her."

They were counting on Miss Sparks being in. Martin had deliberately not phoned her in case her line was being monitored or she got rattled for whatever reason.

Together they walked back to number thirty-seven. Perry figured he must look a sight with his ripped, stained jeans and the crumpled jacket, but perhaps the old dame would think it was fashion.

"So you reckon she knows where this box is?" Martin asked.

"I reckon she's got it. Stands to reason," Perry said. The box had disappeared between Arthur's death and before Sybil's. She hadn't mentioned its absence to Rose, who would surely have been first in line to accuse if it had been stolen. So Sybil must have disposed of it herself.

Likely she felt it might not be safe there, and had perhaps given it to someone else as a form of insurance. If she was blackmailing, and Perry considered this the most likely explanation.

Why anyone would blackmail a killer was beyond Perry. It was like putting your hand in a mousetrap twice. You knew what they were capable of.

Perry had learnt from Jake the Flick what a contract killing was. "King John won't touch them. Far too high stakes and not enough reward. There's always some desperado prepared to have a go for stupidly small cash," he said.

The Company employed more subtle ways to take down those that needed to be taken down. Usually they'd be fitted up and the police sent their way. This wasn't considered informing, perhaps because the police were only being fed false information.

Once or twice Perry caught a hint of something else. Something other than the junkies and failed crims who were prepared to cosh or knife a bloke for a few hundred quid.

Black Bessie, Old Owen, King John and the others of their vintage: they knew something. But whatever it was, it wasn't to be talked of.

"Is there some other lot?" Perry asked Jake once. "Like the Company, but different?"

"You mean the other Chapters? Loads," Jake told him.

"Not like that. I mean something else." Something more secret, more unspoken. Something powerful and sinister.

But Jake claimed he knew nothing. Perry couldn't get anything out of him, though he felt that Jake didn't quite meet his eye.

The one time Perry tried to ask Black Bessie about it he got short shrift. "You've obviously got too much time on your hands if you're filling your head with that kind of rubbish," she said, and gave him some task to do.

It wasn't an answer though. The Company had their secrets, and for now, they weren't Perry's to know.

32

"What is it you want?"

The face that peered at them from behind the chain-locked door had a peevish look about it. Martin did his spiel.

"I'm from Harcourts Solicitors. As you may be aware we've been handling the estate of Mrs Sylvia Stanton, who I believe was a close friend of yours. Could we come in for a short chat?"

There was no response for a few seconds. "I'm very busy this afternoon."

Martin cleared his throat. "It's to do with her will, Miss Sparks." He waited again. "Certain legacies to be disbursed in due course."

The chain was removed. "You'd best come in."

Miss Sparks wasn't much more than fifty, when you looked at her properly, but she had a very old lady air about her. Martin was clean cut and well spoken, and it didn't take more than a few compliments of her pictures, ornaments and Siamese cat for him to successfully butter her up.

Once she had decided she approved of him, not to mention the hints that he might have good news for her, she was only too willing to talk. She had them sit on the sofa in her front room, made them tea, and even put out a plate of biscuits for them.

"As you know the sad circumstances of Mrs Stanton's death have meant a delay in probate. We're also trying to establish some of her other intentions."

"Intentions?" An avaricious light came on in Miss Sparks' eyes.

"It seems she expressed the desire to my uncle to add or adjust some of the details of the bequests in her will. She had more to apportion, of course, following her husband's death. She told us she had drafted some codicils, and was to bring them in for the will to be rewritten. Unfortunately her sudden death prevented this from eventuating."

Perry wondered if there would be any fallout to the web of lies that Martin was spinning. Likely it was Jeff Harcourt who would cop it, not his nephew. The Sparks woman would be in his ear for months demanding her fictitious legacy.

"What was in the codicils?" Miss Sparks asked.

"Naturally we don't know yet, but if they were made in the proper way, they should constitute an actual legal document. A search has been made of Mrs Stanton's home but no such paperwork has turned up. Often in these situations people choose to entrust such paperwork to a reliable friend," Martin said.

Miss Sparks ran the tip of her tongue around her lips. Greed made anyone gullible and stupid, Perry thought. He could see how poor old women were ripe for confidence tricksters.

"I don't suppose she might have entrusted such a thing to you?" Martin asked. "An envelope, perhaps? It may have been forgotten about in all this terrible tragedy."

Perry could tell that Miss Sparks was torn. She knew something but she was probably trying to figure out whether it was to her advantage to reveal it. Curiosity won out.

"She did leave something with me, as it happens. A box of papers. In all the sad business I'd quite forgotten about it until now. Let me fetch it."

Martin caught Perry's eye as Miss Sparks left the room. "She thought there was money in it, most like. That explains her not handing it over to the police. Now she thinks there's a will in it, it's even more valuable to her," he said.

Miss Sparks returned carrying a carved wooden box. She set it down on the coffee table. Perry picked it up. He saw immediately that someone had made an attempt on the lock, likely with a hair pin. Much good would that have done them. It looked like a trick lock, these boxes often had them, not that such a thing made any difference to him.

He wondered why she simply hadn't smashed it open. Not the easiest of tasks, since it was solidly made: proper timber, not plywood. The hinges were glued and screwed so they'd be a job to get off, still doable though. But a few knocks with a mallet and she'd have been inside it. So why not open it?

Perhaps she thought she'd be called to account for it at some point. Or maybe she was biding her time until the will was settled or the investigation was complete and the coast seemed permanently clear. People could be funny like that.

"I'm afraid I don't have a key."

"That's alright, Miss Sparks, we've had a few clients lose the keys to their keepsake boxes," Martin said. "A little bit of wire usually does the trick. Have you got a paperclip?" He would have known that Perry always had tools on him, but it would look suspicious for him to simply bring them out.

"Let me see." She exited again and returned with a couple of paperclips. Martin, having seen what Perry's wires looked like, bent them as closely as possible to the correct shape. He was trying to avoid letting Perry look like an expert, in case this made the woman suspicious.

Martin made a fumbling pretence of trying to open it. "I've not got the knack today. Will you do the honours?" He passed the wires to Perry who opened the box as if he had had the key. "As I mentioned, they're not at all secure, these fancy boxes," Martin said quickly, to assuage any suspicion on Miss Sparks' part.

They opened the box and Martin sifted through. There were, just as Dilys had predicted, a few old photos and a bundle of letters tied in ribbon. No cash or jewellery: Perry saw the disappointment in Miss Sparks' eyes.

Then there was a new, sealed enveloped in a bright shade of light mauve. "This looks the right sort of thing," Martin said, and went to put it in his jacket pocket. But Miss Sparks was having none of that. Denied a fat bundle of notes or a diamond brooch, she was determined to at least have her curiosity assuaged.

"Given dear Sybil entrusted her private papers to me, I couldn't consent to them being taken out of the house without verifying that they weren't of a particularly personal nature," she said.

"Very well." Martin tore the envelope open and drew out a matching mauve paper. It was headed: "Testimony of Sylvia Stanton":

To whom it may concern

I, Sybil Stanton, of The Larches, 18 Iffley Avenue, do testify that on the night of my husband Arthur Stanton's death I saw Frankie Goodlock...

It was the name that Perry expected to see though he knew it would have come as a surprise to Martin. He was impressed by how impassive Martin remained. His face didn't move a muscle.

Instead Martin took calm control of the situation. "This is something unexpected. It looks like you may have solved the murders, Miss Sparks. The police will be very interested in this. If it wasn't for you, carefully taking care of this box..."

It was scant compensation for the loss of her cash and legacy hopes but Miss Sparks had no choice but to make the best of it. She sniffed. "I'm sure it can't be alleged that I did anything to obstruct the course of their duty," she said.

Except conceal obvious evidence for weeks and lie about it, Perry thought. Evidence that would have cleared this up right after Sybil's death and would probably have saved Grover's skin too. But he refrained from pointing this out.

Martin was quick to reassure Miss Sparks that only praise would be coming her way. "Not at all, no one would think that," he said. "The police will be delighted you kept this so safe. I shouldn't wonder if there might be some kind of citizen's award."

This was really laying it on thick with a trowel, Perry thought. The fog of greed gone from her eyes, the woman wasn't that stupid.

"I can wait with you while you call the police," Martin told Miss Sparks. He stood turned to Perry. "You can head back to the office. I just need a quick word." He stood up and went with Perry to the door. Under his breath he said: "We'll get the warrant dropped but it may not be immediate. There's a pub further down the road. I'll meet you there in an hour."

"What if you're not done by then?" Perry asked.

"I will be. I'll call Uncle Jeff and he can take over here. With any luck before she figures out that I'm not actually a lawyer yet."

Martin was burning to know more, Perry could tell, but they were both at risk if Perry stayed too much longer. The police would arrest Perry on sight and Martin would be in trouble for harbouring him.

Once the police had Frankie in their grasp it should all be forgotten, but Perry needed to lie low while the arrest warrant for him remained active.

Martin went back inside Miss Sparks' house to sort out calling the police and his uncle as Perry slipped off.

"I never would have guessed Frankie. I'd put two and two together and come up with Ray."

Martin had managed to meet Perry in the pub as planned. A stiff drink was more than welcome after all that had happened. It was a quiet time of day, being mid-afternoon, and they sat either side of a window table in a nearly empty saloon bar. The sunlight streaming in had gold motes of dust suspended within it. It contrasted with the dark gloom of the furnishings.

Martin gave Perry a brief rundown of what had happened with Miss Sparks and the police, which had consisted of DI Oak and another officer. They'd taken the box off her as well as statements from both her and Martin. "I told them the same line about chasing up Sybil Stanton's documents to settle her estate. They seemed to buy it. I'll have to make sure Uncle Jeff corroborates everything."

DI Oak had also made reference to Perry. "He said if I had heard from my 'other client' or if I expected to - obviously he meant you - then I should advise you to pay them a visit. Turn yourself in, is what he meant. I pointed out that Uncle Jeff's the actual solicitor and all client communications were his domain."

"Do you reckon you got followed here?" Perry asked. He cast his eye around the place. It seemed quiet enough. No one else had entered since Martin's arrival.

"I don't think so. I left her house the other way just in case. Went and sat in that park for ten minutes, then ducked back down the parallel street. Stopped in a newsagent's. I couldn't see anyone, then I slipped in here."

Perry felt strangely emotionless. Not numb. Resigned, perhaps. He'd had longer to get his head around everything than Martin had. Martin still couldn't believe that Frankie had been the target of Sylvia Stanton's blackmailing, and thus the culprit.

"Ray just seemed the most likely suspect. I mean he was there, at the centre of it all," Martin said. "Like a spider in a web."

Perry had given this some thought. "I reckon that was why the call was made from there, to implicate him. But it was obviously Frankie when you put all the facts together. Everything fitted once I realised it was her."

It was Old Owen's remark that had finally triggered the revelation, when he'd talked about the more drought tolerant crops. How they were simply better business sense. This had led Perry to think of Frankie, with her love of money and supposedly a hard head for business, importing useless, unsuitable plants that no one bought, at huge expense. Plants that she was supposedly attached to, but went and sold off for nothing at the Midsummer Festival.

Then there was the time at the barbecue that she suggested she would be only too happy to give up the whole concern. Even at the time it had struck Perry as being out of character but he'd put it down to weariness with the nursery's ongoing financial problems.

There were other things. The fact that both Grover and Sybil Stanton had shown up at the nursery. Frankie's freak-out when Perry had tried to help repot the plants. From that he guessed, and the police would doubtless eventually find it out, that the drugs were hidden around their roots. They had all been succulent types that could take a bit of root disturbance before they wilted.

The chemicals she used in the potting shed too, it was all such an easy and convenient place to cut all the drugs up. Perry remembered from somewhere that boric acid was a common substance used to cut cocaine. Finally there were Frankie's frequent trips to Bristol and all her stress about the delayed plant shipment. No wonder, if it was drugs that she was shipping.

"Do you reckon Barney was involved? Or that he knew?" Martin asked.

"Not a chance." The way Barney had talked about it all, if he'd even had an inkling, he would have been out of there. He wasn't the type for that kind of game.

"I'm glad it wasn't Mary, but she was acting very strangely these past weeks. You've known her for longer than me, you must have noticed?" Martin asked.

"There was a reason for that," Perry said. He wasn't sure if he should say, but it was the kind of thing that would come out eventually. Sooner rather than later, most like. "Dilys says she's expecting. But it's not Ray's."

He gave Martin a close look as he said this. Perry had had a few thoughts as to whether it might have been Martin that Mary had taken up with. After all Martin had been new on the scene, arriving around the time it all must have started.

Martin broke into a smile, momentarily disconcerting Perry. "That explains that, then," he said.

"Explains what?"

"You know who it must be, right?" Martin asked.

Perry had no idea who it was if it wasn't Martin. "I'd wondered if it was you."

Martin laughed. "Not a chance. She's nice enough, but no. You really haven't noticed them mooning after each other?"

"Who?"

"Mary and Barney. They left the Midsummer Festival together. And he's always in there, whenever Mary is and Ray isn't."

Perry was feeling a bit dense now. "I hadn't noticed a thing. Do you suppose Frankie knew?"

"Possibly not. She had other concerns. She might have considered it an advantage if Barney was preoccupied elsewhere. I'm sure Rose must have guessed. It's interesting how she never liked Frankie, did she?"

"Didn't she?" Perry seemed to have been oblivious to a lot of things.

"Rose makes it very clear who she likes. She likes you, of course. And Dilys and Mary. Can't stand Ray. Likes Barney. Pointedly ignores Frankie. Kids get whims like that. It's interesting, nonetheless. Maybe she picked up on something about Frankie that we didn't."

Perry had no idea. He thought it was a good thing if Martin was correct, that Rose hadn't liked Frankie. It would be far easier to find out someone she disliked had murdered her father than someone she trusted.

"So what now then?"

"It depends on how long the police take. We'll do what we can to get the arrest warrant dropped. If I were Uncle Jeff I'd have to advise you to turn yourself in. Since I'm not, feel free to lie low until you're finally cleared. Otherwise you'll be stuck in the cells for as long as they can hold you there. Which isn't that long without charge, but you're not off the hook yet."

Perry thought about it for a while. He watched the thin stream of bubbles rising in his beer, like the golden dust in the shafts of sunlight. There was no way he was handing himself in. He valued every hour of freedom far too much for that.

His greatest fear was that they would botch it up and fail to get the evidence they needed to lock Frankie up, if Sybil Stanton's testimony wasn't considered enough. In which case it might still be pinned on him. Or Frankie might still try to claim that he was working with her and had done the shootings.

There was only one thing to be done, Perry decided. He was going to have to get more evidence himself, and fast. This meant striking out alone and having a snoop of the nursery.

Perry had got used to managing things by himself. He'd had no choice but to become self-reliant, learning as much as he could about narrowboats and life on the water. There was a community there but it was still a solitary life. No one was going to get him out of a fix if he got stuck by himself on a lonely stretch of water.

An old fellow who went by the name of Cap'n Mick had been invaluable in showing him how to turn and steer a narrowboat. You didn't need a licence to pilot one but it still took some skill.

How to operate canal locks had been an education in itself. Perry knew the main thing was to pay attention. He'd seen some horrors happen when people got slack: boats overturned, damaged by lock gates, submerged. Mainly these disasters happened to the less experienced leisure boaters but the river folk weren't immune to errors.

"Anyone can doze off, so you keep your wits about you," Cap'n Mick had told him.

Another bloke had helped him sort out the paperwork he needed. There were fees to pay to the Waterways body, it was all official and legit. You got given keys so you could pass through locks and access some facilities. Perry could have managed without these but it was better to do things properly.

The yard work had taught him plenty about maintenance and some of the mistakes to avoid.

With all this under his belt, and the Emerald nearly ready to take her first proper voyage, he was starting to feel more confident about everything. He'd never have the cocksure spirit of Jake or one like him, but he could hold his own. He no longer felt in thrall to anyone. He could stand up for himself and go his own way.

33

Perry broke into Goodlock Nursery that night. He didn't have to break in since he had a key to the main gate and knew the code for the alarm in the shop. But he didn't want to be seen from the road, so he went via the back and clambered over the fence.

Knowing his way around made it easier, and the just-waning moon cast a good bit of light.

It was a peaceful place at that hour, with all the plants under the dark, empty sky. He headed to the potting shed. It was locked separately because of the chemicals in there, more to prevent a customer from wandering in and making a mess than to stop them stealing anything.

Feeling the familiar buzz in his fingers he picked the shed's lock with wires and pushed the door open.

Perry wasn't quite sure what he was looking for. He increasingly had the thought that Frankie would have cleaned everything up between jobs. All the equipment that she likely used for cutting up the drugs would be the same gear used for measuring out fertiliser chemicals. The quantities required wouldn't even be suspicious. It wasn't like you needed fifty kilos of boric acid to cut a shipment of cocaine. The amount she used would barely make a noticeable dent in their existing stocks.

As he sifted through the place, running his fingers through an open sack of perlite, even sticking his hand in a bucket of organic guano, his hopes were sinking. He knew this must be where she did it, but without the kinds of detection gear that the coppers used, how was he to find any trace?

About the only evidence he found was a small set of scales. Perry knew that Frankie didn't use them for fertiliser because he'd seen her measuring out quantities and the volumes were much larger. Clearly these dainty instruments were for much lighter quantities. That said, Frankie could claim she'd been mixing small, experimental batches of fertiliser. A juror with not much more knowledge beyond garden roses and Miracle-Gro might well be convinced.

Sitting on an upturned crate, Perry considered his options. He couldn't be caught here because breaking in would be another black mark against him. He needed evidence, witnesses.

But dead men tell no tales. Grover was gone, Sybil was gone. And Arthur, who had presumably tumbled to the drugs trafficking even before Frankie started her killing spree.

Yet she'd needed Grover. She hadn't managed the Brewery part alone. So if Grover was out of the picture, how had she managed the latest shipment, that King John and Perry had found?

Someone was working with her. That someone would be able to clear him, if he could persuade them to talk.

The same moment he thought this, he realised in an instant who her accomplice must be. There was no time left to waste.

First thing in the morning, knowing he was risking everything, Perry made his way to the Boatswain.

Mary was already up, looking green about the gills. She looked even paler when she saw him.

"What are you doing here, Perry? Everyone's after you."

"I need to see your brother," he told her.

"Damon? He'll be asleep."

"It's urgent." He saw the worry on her face and held up his hands. "I'm not armed. I didn't do it, any of it."

Mary still looked anxious. "I know that, Perry. It's just we've had the police in here every day. They're probably watching the place. And now Frankie too. They were down here late last night looking for her but they wouldn't tell us anything. What's she got to do with all this?"

Frankie on the loose was not good news. "I don't have much time, then." Perry looked about him. "Where's Ray?" He knew Ray would be on the phone to the coppers as quick as you could blink if he found Perry there.

Mary bit her lip. "He's out. We had a bit of a row last night. He said he was going for a drink in the Stag and walked off and stayed out all night."

That suited Perry. He could do without Ray sticking his oar in. "I really need to speak with Damon," he said.

Mary went to fetch him and Perry waited in the empty bar. Flooded with morning sunlight from the eastern side, it looked bright and innocent. Hardly the scene for drugs and guns and murder suspects.

Damon finally appeared, looking dishevelled. Perry suspected he'd got wasted the previous night and slept in his clothes as usual. He had a nervous, shifty look which reminded Perry of Grover.

"What do you want? Aren't the police out for you?"

"Just a word." Perry flicked his eyes to Mary and back and Damon read his intent. Perry didn't want Mary dragged into this.

"We'll go over here then." Damon led them to one of the corner tables. Mary was looking over at them curiously so Perry kept his voice low.

"I know about Frankie and what was going on down the Brewery. I know you got roped in as well."

Damon started spluttering and trying to deny it. For someone supposedly trained in theatre it was a hopeless performance.

"I need you to tell the coppers everything. I want my name cleared."

The other man looked frightened, his skin a grey-white pallor against the unkempt dark hair. "You've got no proof of anything."

"Frankie will drop you in it the second they catch up with her. And they will. You know they're already after her. Oak's got a written testimony from Sybil Stanton naming Frankie as the person who shot Arthur."

Damon was visibly shaking. "But Sybil's dead..."

Perry was starting to feel irritated. "From before her death. She wrote it down and signed it. Hid it somewhere safe. Sybil was getting hush money from Frankie, that's why she got shot."

"But Frankie didn't do any of the shootings. She said it was likely some rival cartel, if anything. Or something completely unrelated. No one knows about any of the stuff she's doing. It was just a straight up business."

How stupid could Damon be?

"Even if they only pick her up for the drugs, she'll still drop you in it," Perry said.

Before Damon could respond there was a shriek from the bar. They both turned, and saw Mary, clutching her face in horror.

Just through the doorway, standing there with a gun, was Frankie.

"Cosy little discussion you've got going there, boys," she said.

At that moment Rose appeared at the inner door. "Why did you scream?" she asked Mary, and then stopped dead in her tracks, looking at Frankie. Perry never forgot the look on Rose's face.

Swiftly Frankie crossed the room. In a second she had her arm around Rose, twisting the girl's arm behind her back and causing her to cry out, the gun pointed towards her head.

"Anyone tries anything, she gets it."

Mary, who had started inching towards the phone, froze.

Everything was slowing down. The world was in slow motion. Perry found himself noticing every single thing. He was hyper aware. He could hear Mary's fear and Damon's panic even though they were silent. His senses were all mixed up yet enhanced as a result.

"I want the keys to your car, Mary," Frankie said. "Rose won't come to any harm if you just do as I say. If you call the cops, she'll get it."

"You're not taking her with you?" Mary said.

"Shut up and give me your keys."

Rose was looking faint. Mary was rummaging through her bag, frantically. "I can't find them. Ray must have them." Her voice held a sobbing note.

"Don't lie, your car's outside."

"I know, but he took it earlier. Yesterday I mean. Before he went out." Mary was getting confused, panicking. "See?" She tipped out the entire contents of the bag on the floor in front of Frankie and Rose and shook it. Make up, a purse, tissues, pens, other items. She shook it again. No keys.

"You must have a spare."

Mary claimed she didn't. Frankie swore. "Either of you got a car?" she said, turning to Damon and Perry. "No, of course you haven't. Bloody useless, the pair of you."

"What about the van?" Damon said, stuttering his words.

Frankie glared at him. "Every cop car this side of London will be looking for that."

"They're onto you, then?" Perry asked. Amid the crisis he was wondering how and why she had showed up. And why Oak and his men hadn't picked her up the previous evening.

"Thanks to you they paid a little visit last night. Luckily for me, I was out. And then I find half of Thames Valley parked outside our place when I get home this morning. Luckily again, I saw them before they saw me. So I came here. And now I'll be going, or rather we'll be going," she said, indicating the terrified Rose. "Just as soon as one of you sorts out a vehicle for me. If that stupid bitch sister of yours can't find her keys, you'll have to hotwire it. I'm sure Perry will find it no trouble."

Before Perry could respond, there were more arrivals. DI Oak walked through the door with a couple of officers. They were armed but Frankie had a gun to the side of a child's head. They were as helpless as Perry, Mary and Damon.

"Weapons on the floor," Frankie ordered them.

DI Oak nodded to his men and they complied.

It was enough time for Perry. He flicked his eyes to DI Oak who met his look in return. Perry's hand closed over the ashtray on the table that he and Damon were sitting at.

In a lightning fast motion he flung it at the window on the side of the room, smashing the glass. The noise caused Frankie to turn, momentarily pointing the gun in its direction. As nimble as a cat Perry sprang across the room, grabbing Rose and throwing her to the floor, shielding her with his body.

At the same time Oak had rushed on Frankie and was now grappling with her, twisting her arm up to the ceiling and forcing the pistol to discharge.

Then it was all over very quickly. Handcuffs and a furious, abusive Frankie being bundled into a police car. A woman police officer taking charge of Rose who was clinging to Perry like a vine.

Mary collapsed, clutching her stomach and someone radioed for an ambulance.

Perry was taken down to the police station. He wasn't even aware whether he was being escorted or arrested but he didn't care. They had her. Rose was safe. Bruised probably, but otherwise physically uninjured.

But far more vivid than anything that had just happened were the memories of Jake and the gunshot. Flashing through Perry's mind with his racing heartbeat. The past eclipsing the present.

And he heard it again and again and again. The same gunshot.

Jake's death was the main reason he never went back. Perry had gone all the years since with a part of him imagining that maybe Jake was still out there somewhere. To go back would force him to acknowledge that Jake was gone.

Later on it seemed more like it happened another lifetime than just a few years ago.

Perry had never been into violence, nor had Jake. Jake's knife was a tool and sometimes a threat, but he'd never cut anyone that Perry knew of. He'd even avoided getting into situations where it would be necessary.

For a cop to pull a gun on him and not even give him a chance, it was like murder. A knife against a gun, and Jake wasn't even wielding his knife. He was defenceless.

Except the gun hadn't been aimed at him. It had been pointed at Perry, until Jake threw himself between them.

The gunshot: he fell.
The gunshot: he fell.
The gunshot: he fell.
Crumpled. Slumped. Broken.
Jake, who had sacrificed himself for Perry.

All over. You couldn't come back from that. You couldn't turn the clock back. You could have all the power in the world and there was nothing, nothing, nothing you could do.

Too late. It was too late.

And what was the point of anything, if life was so fragile and so cheap?

34

Funny how a day ago he was prime suspect and now they were talking about some hero award. Not that Perry planned to stick around any longer, now he was finally cleared and free to go.

The atmosphere in the Boatswain was surreal. He went there because the canal side offered no peace. It was crawling with reporters trying to interview him, their photographers snapping endless photos of the Emerald.

Mary wasn't there, she was still in hospital but apparently her pregnancy was okay. It hadn't been a great way for Frank to find out. The pub was absolutely packed with sticky beaks flocking to visit the scene of the crime. And more press, of course. Perry was sick of them and wouldn't speak to any of them. He let Martin handle them.

Dilys was now taking care of Rose and had moved into the pub for a couple of nights. Damon had disappeared so Dilys had taken his room.

No one really cared about Damon. The police would pick him up soon enough. He wasn't smart enough to evade them for long.

Barney had hardly known whether he was coming or going. After the police had finally finished with him for that day he'd headed to the hospital to be with Mary. "One moment his wife turns out to be a drug trafficking murderer. The next he finds out he's going to be a father," Dilys said. She was the only one who seemed to be taking everything in her stride, regarding it all with her usual wry detachment.

Even Martin was shaken up. It had all been a bit of a game to him. Something to regard from a distance, going through clues like a crossword puzzle. Except it was real life. A real person he had sat and drank with and never suspected had turned out to be a cold blooded killer. He didn't say much about it, but Perry sensed his chagrin.

Priscilla was all over Perry again. She'd been giving interviews to the newspapers all day even though Martin had cautioned her not to. "Pretty Barmaid's Gunpoint Hostage Horror" would be all over the front pages tomorrow, even though she hadn't even been there. Perry found himself wondering what he had ever seen in her.

Rose sat with them, even though she wasn't supposed to be in the pub at that hour. Given what she'd been through, she needed to be with people she felt safe with. She said nothing all night, just sipped her lemonade through a straw and didn't even eat the crisps Dilys gave her.

"The social workers wanted to take her but I reckoned that would make things worse. You'll be alright after a good sleep, won't you, love? It'll all seem better in the morning, and we'll go and visit Mary." Dilys lit another cigarette. She had given up her plans to quit smoking for now, and said she'd try again in the new year.

Perry understood better now why Jake had done what he had done. The guilt had wracked him for years. Until he himself had felt that visceral urge to protect a smaller, weaker being. He wasn't sure if it lessened his guilt at being the one who survived, but it made it easier to bear.

"I never suspected Frankie," Dilys said. "But then I never cleaned for her. If I had done I've have sussed it out weeks ago. People give away all sorts when you start clearing up their messes for them."

Perry thought about Frankie. She must have been a good actress, to take Barney in for so long. They'd met in South America, he remembered. Had she thought of the plant importing scheme before she met him, or had his background been a lucky break?

He remembered her at the Midsummer Festival. The supposedly peace-loving hippy with her braids and tattoos, selling "mystical" organic plants. The real reason being to dump the old stock as quickly as possible so she had an excuse to import the next load.

DI Oak had taken Perry aside at the station before he left. Not an official interview, just a chat. Perry had been desperate to get out of the place and resented being held back.

"I read up on the raid you got done for," DI Oak told Perry. "Partly routine, partly out of curiosity."

He had got them both a tea from the vending machine but Perry wasn't drinking his. He sat there, impassive, wanting to wall it off. He didn't need Oak raking it all up again.

DI Oak had a file with him. He put it on the table and opened it in front of Perry, leafing through some documents.

"The officer who fired the shot. Sergeant Daniel Watts, twenty-four years old, brand new to the firearms unit. He was suspended pending an investigation. He never made it back to the force, he had a breakdown a few months later. Two years after the shooting he took his own life."

He tapped a section of the paper.

"Same age as your mate Jake. One mistake. One mix-up. One nervous, inexperienced officer, out of his depth. Two lives lost as a result."

Oak pushed the file towards Perry though Perry didn't read it. What was the point?

"It should never have happened of course, though I realise it's too late to say that now. The senior officers running the squad did face disciplinary proceedings. Procedures were also changed after that. Other than your friend, Thames Valley Police has only had to use a firearm against somebody once in its entire history."

Like any of it mattered. Perry simply wanted to get away from it all. From the police, the whole place.

Yet he now shared a reluctant bond with Oak. The detective had read his intentions in a split second. Their moves had been coordinated even though neither of them knew how. Luck? Instinct? Random chance?

Side-by-side, Perry had worked with the police in that final crisis. He had saved Rose and Oak had got Frankie. Everyone safe because they'd simultaneously taken action.

"The jobs you're doing for Harcourts," DI Oak began.

Perry braced himself for a ticking off and a warning.

"It's not a bad line of business to be in. There's a lot of work there, much of it legitimate. You could do well for yourself," DI Oak said.

Perry looked at him, sensing he was being patronised, but Oak met his eyes as an equal. There was respect there.

It took Perry aback. He would have been more comfortable to see the usual contempt that the scuffers showed towards the likes of him.

He needed to get away, to make a move. It was all starting to be too much to take.

When Perry finally got the engine fixed it became something of a celebration. He hadn't realised how closely many of the other boat people and those at the yard had been following his progress.

"You'll have to christen her," he was told. "Have you got a name for her?"

The boat's old name had long worn off, but the farmer had told him it was "Riverview". Perry felt little compunction about changing this. It wasn't like he was erasing some other woman's name.

By chance, much of the paint he'd scavenged had been a dark green. Or perhaps not by chance, since it was a popular colour on the waterways. He'd also got hold of some red paint to offset it, trying to copy the colour schemes he saw on other boats.

The boat yard owner surprised Perry with a bottle of champagne to smash against the boat. Several of them had chipped in for it. Another, who was a skilled signwriter, had painted "The Emerald" in beautifully styled lettering on the bow.

No one had done stuff like this for Perry before and he was pleased but embarrassed. He didn't know how he could thank them.

"Just watching you succeed in bringing an old beauty back to the waterways has been reward enough," one of them told him.

Not really knowing what to do once the champagne was broken over the Emerald to a chorus of cheers, Perry got onto the boat and started her up. He unhooked her from the moorings and began his first proper voyage down the river.

Perry was properly one of the water folk now. A liveaboard, as they called them. The Emerald was no longer a dumb boat, stuck bobbing at a mooring. They were on the move. Together they could cruise the waterways, the length and breadth of the land if Perry wanted to. The world was his.

35

Perry was ready. It was nearly September, the summer would soon be over.

There was nothing to keep him here. Nearly everyone was leaving.

Mary and Barney planned to move away and start over somewhere else. The place held bad memories for both of them and there was the kid on the way to think of. They were keen to get away and put it all behind them. To begin again, maybe with the market garden that Barney had been dreaming of.

Ray was also selling up. Not so much due to the split with Mary, but because he'd got himself into some hot water over a married woman he'd been seeing. Her husband wasn't so much the problem as her sister, whom Ray had also been having a go with.

Priscilla was going back to her family in Basingstoke. She said she planned to look for a job in London. Martin was also heading to London but had no plans to remain in touch with Priscilla, as much as she hinted at it.

Damon was still on the run but wasn't likely to get much of a sentence, it being a first offence and his involvement being relatively minor. What he'd do and where he would afterwards was anyone's guess Perry had a fair idea that Barney wouldn't be providing him free board with him and Mary. Likely Damon would drift off somewhere, and eventually get into more trouble.

As planned, Rose was going to live with her relatives in the north. Dilys was taking her up there by train and stopping by to see some relatives on the way back. She and Rose came down to the canal to wish Perry farewell.

Rose still didn't want to move away but she didn't make a scene about it. She was putting on a brave face, and it made her look even younger and more frightened.

"Mary says it will be nice up there, but I won't know anyone, will I?"

Dilys tried to reassure her. "You'll soon make new friends, once you start school. You can always come back and visit."

"Everyone's leaving though," Rose said.

She'd lost her father, her home, her friends. Perry felt bad for her. "You can get all over the country by boat. Maybe I'll sail up your way one day," he said.

There was hope in her eyes at this. "I know you didn't believe me about the box. I suppose I got it wrong about Sybil," she said. "But then you did go and find it, and they wouldn't have caught her if it weren't for you. And you saved my life, Perry Beck."

He nearly forgot that he had something for her. It wasn't much of a souvenir, but it was something he had promised her. "Here you are."

He handed Rose a matchbox and she took it, curious. Inside it was a fishing fly, a traditional one for angling with a barbed hook, not one of the butterfly-style jewellery flies he'd made for the festival. Perry had wound it with green and blue threads, to give it an iridescent look, like a bluebottle. The hook was tipped with cork.

"Can I fish with it?" Rose asked. "Is it a real one?"

"If you take the cork off, yes," Perry told her.

"I won't though. A fish might eat it and get away with it," she said.

Perry laughed. "You do what you like with it, Rosie."

He had already undone the Emerald's bow line and stern line from the moorings, and lifted the fenders ready to go. Pushing out the vessel as he stepped on, he went to start the engine.

The narrowboat moved off in a smooth glide. It was a gentle departure, the way a boat quietly slipped away. When Perry reached the bend in the canal he turned back and waved at them one last time. They both waved back, and then they were lost from sight.

Perry was on his own again. New adventures awaited.

About Edward Turbeville

Edward Turbeville is a mystery writer from England's ancient Forest of Dean.

His favourite authors include Agatha Christie, Evelyn Waugh, P G Wodehouse and Nevil Shute.

Edward is also a fan of the Classics, notably Cicero and Vergil, and he has published an alliterative verse translation of Book III of the Aeneid.

His website is: **http://www.edwardturbeville.com**

You can also sign up for Edward's mailing list at: **http://www.subscribepage.com/edward**

www.ingramcontent.com/pod-product-compliance
Lightning Source LLC
Chambersburg PA
CBHW072258130726
47910CB00012B/2152